SHERLOCK HOLMES
MYSTERY MAGAZINE
VOL. 7, NO. 3   **Issue #24**

STAFF

Publisher: John Betancourt
Editor: Marvin Kaye
Non-fiction Editor: Carla Coupe
Assistant Editor: Steve Coupe

Sherlock Holmes Mystery Magazine is published by Wildside Press, LLC. Single copies: $10.00 + $3.00 postage. U.S. subscriptions: $59.95 (postage paid) for the next 6 issues in the U.S.A., from: Wildside Press LLC, Subscription Dept. 7945 MacArthur Blvd, Suite 215, Cabin John, MD 20818. International subscriptions: see our web site at www.wildsidepress.com. Available as an ebook through all major ebook etailers, or our web site, www.wildsidepress.com.

COMING NEXT TIME...

STORIES! ARTICLES!
SHERLOCK HOLMES & DR. WATSON!

Sherlock Holmes Mystery Magazine #25
is just a few months away...watch for it!

FROM WATSON'S NOTEBOOKS

As ever, my friend Holmes is looking forward to the next issue of *Sherlock Holmes Mystery Magazine* because its contents will be devoted wholly to his adventures. Meanwhile, the current number includes my report on the crooked man. In the nonfiction section, our regular contributor Bruce Kilstein, M D, discusses my literary agent Conan Doyle's doings as a medical practitioner, which you may know is how he began his career.

—John H Watson, M D

✗ ✗ ✗ ✗

In addition to Dr. Kilstein, three regulars appear in these pages: Teel James Glenn, Laird Long, and Dianne Neral Ell. Di, as I like to call her, wrote an excellent "caper" novel, *The Exhibit*, which the publisher forced her to cut more than they should have. I am pleased to report that an expanded version has been reissued.

Marion McMahon Stanley makes her first appearance here and the issue also includes a new Nero Wolfe story, in which the Great Detective defends none other than Inspector Cramer. And in the tradition of John Dickson Carr's fat sleuth H.M., who turned defense counsel in *The Judas Window*, so does Mr. Wolfe in a courtroom drama presided over by a distaff judge based on a real New York City woman who gave an inspiring lecture on women's rights in the mystery class I once taught at New York University.

Issue # 25 will feature both a new Holmes story and an article about Dr. Watson by Gary Lovisi and other Canonical tales by Paul Hearns, Bradley Harper and Jim Robb.

Canonically Yours,
Marvin Kaye

✗

ASK MRS HUDSON

by (Mrs) Martha Hudson

Dear Mrs Hudson,
   What were your first impressions of Sherlock Holmes?
   Miss Laura O'Connor

⚔   ⚔   ⚔

Dear Miss O'Connor,
   Oh, dear! I am afraid that my initial opinion of him was somewhat negative. I found him truculent to the point of rudeness and was about to turn him down as a tenant when he surprised me by commenting on so many details of my past, as well as activities I'd recently been involved in. I was sure he'd been spying on me, but then he explained with uncharacteristic patience how he knew so much about me wholly through what he called "the science of deduction." I decided to accept him as the new occupant of the B apartment and I am glad I did so, especially since his companion Dr Watson was the most courtly gentleman I'd ever met.
   Sincerely,
   Martha Hudson

⚔   ⚔   ⚔   ⚔

Dear Mrs Hudson,
   Some time ago when you were out of town caring for your ailing aunt, a Mrs Warren filled in for you and even wrote a column for this magazine.
   I wonder whether you and she are still in touch with one another. I trust that she is well?
   With some concern,
   Florinda Chapman

⚔   ⚔   ⚔

Dear Florinda Chapman,
   That is ever so caring of you. I have passed along your sentiments to Mrs Warren and she thanks you and said to assure you that she is not only well, she recently remarried and is about to visit

America with her new husband. They will spend their honeymoon in New York, where she hopes to see a performance of Mr Gillette's Sherlock Holmes play.

Appreciatively,
Martha Hudson

✗   ✗   ✗   ✗

Mrs Hudson,
Now that Mr Holmes has retired, do you ever see him?
Grant Merritt

✗   ✗   ✗

Dear Mr Merritt,
I regret that I have not seen him for a few years as he has moved away and is busy raising and managing bees. He does write to me occasionally, but has never invited me to visit, though I am sure that is only a matter of absent-mindedness (if such is possible in such a formidable brain!).

I do see Dr Watson fairly often. He still maintains his medical practice and since he is again a widower, he lives in rooms behind his office. It was only a few days ago that he dropped by and invited me to have dinner with him. We did so and enjoyed catching up with one another, as they say. He revealed that he (ever the romantic) is hoping to meet someone who might be interested in marriage. I told him with utter candor that he surely will be successful as he is a most attractive gentleman.

Sincerely,
Martha Hudson

✗   ✗   ✗   ✗

Dear Mrs Hudson,
With Mr Holmes retired, do you know how that has affected Inspector Lestrade?
L. T. Cramer, NYPD

✗   ✗   ✗

Dear Inspector Cramer,
Yes, I have read about you in several books by Mr Rex Stout. Lestrade has also retired, but now that he is a widower he has moved to—guess where? Right here in my B apartment where Mr

Holmes used to live. He even invited Dr Watson to share his old "digs" with him, but that is unlikely to occur.

It is interesting to have witnessed how Mr Lestrade changed over the years. Though he often appreciated Mr Holmes's help, he behaved toward him, I thought, rather superciliously at best, dismissively at worst. But with the years, they both mellowed and became quite fond of one another. As for the good doctor, he and Lestrade often dine together.

Sincerely,

Martha Hudson

✗ ✗ ✗ ✗

Dear Mrs Hudson,

In the course of your dealings with Mr Holmes, I wonder whether you ever became involved in a court case?

Curiously,

Phileas Fogg (Esq)

✗ ✗ ✗

Dear Mr Fogg,

On a few occasions, I was called as a witness in cases that came about due to Mr Holmes, and there was one time that involved me to a much greater extent, but I am wary of sharing details about it, for I have ascertained that you are the grandson of the Fogg who was part of the legal firm of Dodson and Fogg. Because of their negative reputation, I feel I must communicate with you no further. I tender my regrets if I am being overly cautious.

Yrs truly,

(Mrs) M Hudson

✗ ✗ ✗ ✗

As you know, I like to end my columns with recipes for food that I have served to Mr Holmes and Dr Watson. Following is a delicious meal equally good in warm or chilly weather.

HAM AND FIGS

1 cooked ham
Steamed dried figs

¼ cup of fig juice
¼ cup of brown sugar mixed with ground cloves

1. Brush the ham with the sugar and cloves.

2. Place in a pan and bake at 325 degrees for 20 minutes per pound.

3. Once the sugar has liquified, pour the fig juice on it and baste every 20 minutes.

4. If the mixture sticks to the pan, add a little juice, either grapefruit, orange, or pineapple.

5. Festoon halved figs on the ham 45 minutes before it is done cooking.

THE GRAND MADAME

by Mackenzie Clarkes

Clanging of cups
Clanking of
Silver dishes
On steel trays
Her aged feet
Pressing on creaky
Floorboards
As she
Climbs to her
Boarder's rooms.

SCREEN OF THE CRIME

by Kim Newman

This month, I'm looking at some Sherlockian cinema from around the world.

Migel Faria Jr.'s Brazilian *O Xangô de Baker St* (*A Samba for Sherlock*) (2001) and José Luis Garci's Spanish *Holmes & Watson. Madrid Days* (2012) have many points of similarity. Both find an unusually romantic Holmes and a bearded Watson in Latin countries on the bloody trail of Jack the Ripper, prefiguring Whitechapel atrocities in Brazil and following them up in Spain. In neither case does the great detective unmask a culprit or save anyone—indeed, he spends more time as a regular tourist than showing off his customary genius. Both movies spend a great deal of time on local history and politics, rope in a few contemporary celebrities, and highlight Holmes's musical interests—though Faria's film, from a novel by Jo Soares, is essentially comic with satirical jabs at the absurdities of the well-loved characters and Garci's—scripted by the director, Maria San Roman Riveiro and Andrea Tenuta from a story by Eduardo Torres-Dulce, is rather melancholy in tone, suspended somewhere between *Murder By Decree* and *Mr. Holmes*. Joaquim de Almeida and Gary Piquer are unlikely to be listed among the great screen Sherlocks, but both do distinctive, even unusual things with the role. Both films break with their fairly lavish, respectable, classy moods to include extremely graphic violent imagery … and are populated by beautiful, striking, exotic actresses who aren't treated especially well, though Maria de Medeiros and Bélen López are splendid as Sarah Bernhardt and Irene Adler respectively.

O Xangô de Baker St is a sumptuous period piece, a knockabout comedy at the expense of Conan Doyle's stuffy heroes and a gruesome serial killer thriller all done up in one package. In 1886, Rio de Janiero high society is aghast at the theft of a rare Stradivarius violin from Countess Maria Luiza (Claudia Abreu)—mostly because it seems to have been a love token from Emperor Dom Pedro

II (Claudio Marzo) to the glamorous widow. Sarah Bernhardt (de Medeiros), who is touring South America, suggests the Emperor consult her personal friend, the great English detective Sherlock Holmes (de Almeida). A group of radical abolitionists—Brazil would not end slavery for another twenty years—who cluster in the bookshop of Miguel Lara (Caco Ciocler) are more concerned that the masked violin thief is stalking the streets, strangling young women with the strings of the instrument and playing an air on the remaining strings as he escapes the police. Holmes, who knows Portuguese, arrives with the strictly English-speaking Watson (Anthony O'Donnell) and vaguely concerns himself with the case (he invents the term 'serial killer'), though he is easily distracted by a young samba singer (Thalma de Freitas), who persuades him to exchange cocaine for cannabis.

Eventually clues lead the detective to a voodoo-style ceremony where Watson is briefly possessed by a female spirit who gives unhelpful advice. The whodunit angle is dropped late in the day with a sudden reveal of the guilty party and a surprisingly straight gruesome murder, though Holmes never notices who the killer is—and an inevitable epilogue reveals that the violin player is now working in Whitechapel. There is grotesque humor, as Holmes, Watson, a policeman, and the coroner juggle the liver of the latest victim in the morgue while her grieving father has a histrionic fit, but much of the comedy comes from Holmes setting fashions in Rio, exchanging his sombre tweeds for an all-white linen version of his usual outfit and inventing the caipirinha cocktail. Handsome de Almeida (whose English language roles include *Desperado*, *24*, and *Fast Five*) plays Holmes as a clumsy dolt whose deductions are mostly off the mark (he fails to spot a vital clue because he has learned Portuguese but not *Brazilian* Portuguese) and gets arrested for public indecency with his samba girlfriend Ana (Thalma de Freitas), but he also has a fine duelling violins sequence (with the Bach Double Violin and Solo Piano concerto) with one of the suspects. It benefits from period musical numbers, lovely costumes, historical footnotes, and quite a lot of silly charm (Watson possessed by a flirty female demon)—but is a little overlong and the ending feels oddly sour.

Madrid Days finds Holmes (Piquer) having something of a midlife crisis, dallying with a not-yet-divorced Irene (López) while

Watson (José Kuis Garcia Pérez) is newly married to the former Mary Morstan (Leticia Dolera) and getting on with his life. In Baker Street, Mrs Hudson is just a voice responding to the detective's incessant demands and it still rankles that Jack the Ripper got away. Meeting with Inspector Abberline (Juan Calot), they rattle through the usual suspects—Sickert, Druitt, Gull, etc.—and rule them out, also ridiculing Masonic conspiracies and government cover-ups…which leaves them with nothing, save the fact that a copycat murder spree is underway in Madrid. Watson agrees to leave his happy home to accompany Holmes to Spain, where they team up with Inspector Valcárcel (Enrique Villén)—whose name Watson can never remember—and crusading red-headed journalist Josita Alcántra (Victor Clavijo), who has his own complicated backstory and is in a relationship with bespectacled can-can dancer Berna (Macarena Gómez). Victims with the same initials as the women in Whitechapel keep being killed, but Holmes doesn't seem to apply himself to the case, as if he's already admitted defeat.

For all the pooh-poohing of government conspiracies and the like, this does come round to suggesting that the murders—similar clutches have been committed in several countries—serve a political purpose, and that the killer is both aided and opposed by high-placed characters with shadowy connections. In several scenes Holmes nods sagely as monologues are delivered about the changes in turn-of-the-century society but the film oddly never follows through with concrete revelations or even much in the way of plot development. In a sub-plot, Watson has a harmless flirtation with an aristocrat (Manuela Velasco) but stays faithful to Mary … this Spanish film seems to think that romantic and intellectual timidity is a particularly English vice, and uses the characters of Watson and Holmes to embody them. Irene, an American, gets to critique Holmes at length for his failings as a man—though the characters seem on the verge of a mature relationship near the end, which is all very well but not much help for the poor women who get dissected to prove a point. Among the local celebrities—off-limits as suspects, of course—featured are the novelist Benito Pérez Galdós (Carlos Hipólito) and composer Isaac Albéniz (Alberto Ruiz Gallardón, Albéniz's great-nephew).

Like the Brazilian film, this is at least as concerned with recreating a particular era in a particular city as having Holmes and

Watson hunt Jack the Ripper … again, lovely costumes, locations, sets, and faces evoke a *belle epoque* that was still littered with cut-up women and on the point of losing its veneer of polite charm and becoming a ruthless 20th century ("evil is the engine of the future," diagnoses Holmes). Also, at a tad over two hours, it suffers from *longeurs*, and viewers of a Holmesian persuasion may be frustrated by the way criminal mysteries are set aside in favor of slightly muddled meditations on the turning of the century and the unlocking of Holmes's heart.

✗

Kim Newman is a prolific, award-winning English writer and editor, who also acts, is a film critic, and a London broadcaster. Of his many novels and stories, one of the most famous is *Anno Dracula*.

COP ROCK:

SUCCESS OF A FAILURE

by Eugene D. Goodwin

In 1990 the most unusual police procedural in TV history aired for a very short time. Only seven episodes were shown, although eleven were filmed. Since then *Cop Rock* has become virtually iconic. It was the brainchild of the estimable Steven Bochco, who did much better with his other police series, *Hill Street Blues* and *NYPD Blues*.

Not only were the reviews bad, but public opinion also was quite negative to the extent that Bochco says they never tuned in to give it a chance because they hated the idea of the series so much.

What idea could be so offensive? Everyone thought Bochco had gone mad because though both dramatic and tough, *Cop Rock* was also a musical! The first episode features five songs by Randy Newman, who sings the theme song during the opening credits.

If more people had given it a chance they would have realized, at least, that both the stories and the characters were extremely well written. The cast included such veterans as Ann Bobby, Barbara Bosson as the Mayor of Los Angeles, Ronny Cox as Police Chief Kendrick, as well as Dennis Lipscomb, Vondie Curtis-Hall, Larry Joshua, Peter Onorati, Teri Austin, and many other excellent actors.

While each episode has its own storyline, a few continue through several installments and one develops in every one of the eleven shows—a policeman shoots and kills a criminal who the day before murdered a policeman.

The musical numbers range from gentle ballads through rap and other forms and in the very first show, a scene in a courtroom has the jury declaring its verdict in a stirring gospel number. Some of the music includes choreography.

Recently the DVD was released of the complete series with interviews with Ann Bobby and Steven Bochco. See for yourself why a core of fans have championed *Cop Rock* over the years.

Very highly recommended!

Gene Goodwin is a fan of Colorado, since that's where he learned to love TexMex food.

THE LOVELY CASTOR BEAN

by O'Neill Curatolo

Mr. Sherlock Holmes was an expert in the poisons of his time and even carried out forensic chemistry research in his Baker Street rooms. Regardless, his solution of poison-related murder cases generally pivoted on macroscopic diagnostic procedures such as smelling the corpse's lips, as in *A Study in Scarlet*, or observing a corpse's alkaloid-induced tetanic grin, the *risus sardonicus*, as in *The Sign of the Four*. The drugs involved were typically described no more specifically than "a powerful vegetable alkaloid" or "some strychnine-like substance." Of course, this predated the advent of forensic laboratories and the explosion of biochemical knowledge that occurred later in the 20th Century. The array of tools available for the deceitful murderer today would no doubt fascinate Holmes, though luckily the products of 20th and 21st Century biochemistry and cell biology are generally just outside the available reach of those with a near-term desire to kill. Ah, but those with time and the right resources have a wonderful new toolkit!

Consider, for example, the beautiful castor bean, from the plant *Ricinus communis*. About the breadth of a fingernail, it has a hard, shiny, black-and-brown mottled shell whose beauty has enticed generations of admirers to string these beans together to make necklaces. Unfortunately, from time to time, an unlucky child has chewed one of these necklaced beads and has become very ill— and occasionally worse. For the castor bean holds a secret in its interior: the potent poison ricin.

In 1976, when I was a biochemistry graduate student, I became interested in plant proteins called lectins, which could bind red blood cells together. These proteins attached to the red cell surface membrane and crosslinked red cells to each other, forming an agglutinated mass. I was interested in using plant lectins to probe the structure and function of cell membranes in general, and after perusing the scientific literature on the subject, decided to isolate the lectin from *Ricinus communis*, called, not surprisingly, *Ricinus communis* agglutinin (RCA).

As protein isolations go, this was relatively straightforward, and in a late part of the procedure I used a chromatography method to separate RCA from a similar contaminant protein called ricin. I saved the RCA, and poured the ricin down the drain. Little did I know that at approximately the same time, probably in Russia, another equally earnest young biochemist was carrying out a similar isolation, but saving the ricin and discarding the RCA.

About one year later, on September 7, 1978, a forty-nine-year-old Bulgarian dissident named Georgi Markov was waiting for a bus near Waterloo Bridge in London, when he felt a sting in the back of his right thigh. He noticed a man pick up his umbrella from the ground and rush off. Within hours, Mr. Markov became ill and was taken to St. James' Hospital, Balham, where a puncture bruise in his thigh was noted. He exhibited multiple confusing symptoms, rapidly declined, and died three days after his injury.

On autopsy, a 1.5 mm diameter sphere was removed from the puncture wound in his thigh. Scientists at the Government Chemical Defence Establishment at Porton Down concluded that the pellet delivered ricin, based on the small dose possible in the tiny sphere, Mr. Markov's symptoms and rapid death, and the known high toxicity of ricin. It was not possible to isolate or identify any residual poison from the sphere utilizing late 1970s technology.

While the attacker was never identified, the authorities generally concluded that Mr. Markov had been injected using a weaponized umbrella by the Bulgarian Secret Police to silence his dissident radio broadcasts. Years later, former Russian KGB agent defectors confirmed KGB involvement in the assassination.

When I read about the Markov case, I vowed that I would wear rubber gloves and take other precautions if I ever isolated castor bean proteins again.

The record on assassination attempts similar to the Markov case is sketchy at best. While it has been purported that six other ricin pellet injection attacks occurred in the 1970s-1980s, public evidence is lacking. In one case, a CIA/KGB double agent claimed to have been injected with a poisonous pellet in Tyson's Corner, Virginia. This was followed by a high fever and delirium. There are multiple inconsistent accounts of this case and no public investigation has ever been described.

A more famous case did not involve an injected pellet, but has been purported to involve a skin prick with a gel containing ricin. In 1971, the Russian dissident Alexander Solzhenitsyn was in a grocery in the town of Novocherkassk when a KGB agent surreptitiously exposed him, probably superficially on his skin. Solzhenitsyn was not aware of being pricked, but felt skin discomfort on the left side of his body as the day progressed and developed skin blisters by the next morning. He developed a high fever and agonizing pain and was sick for two to three months. A physician observed that Solzhenitsyn's symptoms were consistent with skin poisoning by ricin.

So what is ricin and why is it so toxic?

The castor plant *Ricinus communis* is grown commercially and the beans are pressed to produce castor oil, which is non-toxic and has a wide variety of medical and non-medical applications. The press-cake left after oil isolation contains the protein ricin, and is toxic if eaten (as is the intact bean). There are numerous reports of horse, cattle, and poultry fatalities from unintentional and intentional press-cake poisoning.

Oral consumption by humans of the castor bean press-cake, or of isolated ricin, results primarily in local gastrointestinal (GI) effects—severe diarrhea and vomiting. Because ricin is a protein, its molecular size is too large to be absorbed across the intestinal wall and thus little or no ricin can reach the bloodstream. Furthermore, the GI tract contains enzymes that degrade dietary proteins into amino acids that can be absorbed as nutrients.

The protein ricin also undergoes such digestion after oral dosing as if it were a dietary protein, and consequently, only a small amount of the protein is available for a brief period of time to poison the cells of the GI wall. Regardless, this is enough to wreak havoc and the victim may die if diarrhea-induced dehydration is not dealt with. Modern hospitals are well-equipped with the knowledge to deal with dehydration and the reinstatement of proper electrolyte balance, as is typically done for diseases such as cholera and ebola. If an orally-dosed ricin victim is hospitalized quickly, the prognosis today is generally good.

If ricin is injected under the skin or directly into the bloodstream, the situation is very different. The toxic protein will rapidly travel through the lymph and bloodstream to almost all organs of the body.

In a conceptual way, one may think of the ricin molecule as resembling a tiny football. At one end, the so-called "Ricin B-Chain" is a Trojan horse of sorts, which binds to cell surfaces, facilitating ingress of the entire protein into the interior of the cell. The other end of the tiny football, the so-called "Ricin A-Chain," is the business part of the protein, which once inside the cell inactivates ribosomes, which are the biochemical machines that carry out protein synthesis within the cell.

This inactivation occurs by cleavage of a specific chemical bond in one of the biopolymers that make up the structure of the ribosome. One ricin molecule can permanently inactivate 1500 ribosomes per minute, quickly shutting down manufacture of all the proteins the cell needs to thrive and survive. The cell quickly dies. Because ricin possesses a generally promiscuous Trojan horse capability, it can bind to most cell types in the body, dragging the deadly protein into cells of the kidney, liver, heart, and virtually all organs.

This is catastrophic and irreversible. What a dastardly design!

Thus, from a medical perspective, the toxicity of ricin is much greater after injection, as the toxin has easy access to almost all organs of the body. The median lethal dose (LD50) of ricin is about 20 micrograms per kilogram body weight when dosed by injection and about 1 milligram per kilogram body weight when swallowed.

For a 70 kilogram (155 pound) human, these values correspond to a total dose of 1.4 milligrams when injected and 70 milligrams when swallowed. To put this in perspective, 1.4 milligrams is about the size of a pinhead. Potent stuff!

Now the teleological question—why does ricin exist? In general, plant toxins likely exist to protect the plant from predators. In the case of the castor plant, the toxin is present in the leaves and the seeds, and is known to be poisonous to aphids and various types of plant-boring worms.

In Doyle's *The Sign of the Four*, a blow-pipe was used to fire an alkaloid-soaked thorn into a victim's scalp. Over one hundred years later, with more potent biologic poisons, this general approach appears to still be viable.

✗

O'Neill Curatolo is a biophysicist who holds 36 U.S. Patents. His suspense novel *Campanilismo* (2013) chronicles the activities of drug industry physicians and scientists in ethically murky waters in New Jersey, Kuala Lumpur, and Malaysian Borneo. A sequel titled *Too Many Hats* will be released in 2018.

CONAN DOYLE, HOLMES, WATSON, AND MEDICINE

by Bruce Kilstein, D.O., F.A.C.O.S.

In *A Study in Scarlet* (1887) Dr. Arthur Conan Doyle introduces his reader to Dr. John Watson who invites us to share his narrative of the adventures of Sherlock Holmes. The love affair between reader and Doyle's creation, still strong after 130 years, begins with Watson's medical discharge from the military. Upon returning to the "cesspool" of London, Watson realizes that he will require a roommate in a city too expensive for an unemployed, invalid physician. An acquaintance introduces Watson to Holmes in the chemistry lab of St. Bart's Hospital where Holmes is on the verge of developing a breakthrough test for the presence of human hemoglobin. Watson and reader are then pulled into the life of the detective as we plunge down the rabbit hole to glimpse a dark side of London, of humanity, rarely seen by the layman. From the outset, we are drawn into a tale of medicine and forensics following a doctor following Holmes as he astonishes police with his ability to tease subtle clues from minute observations of crime scenes. Holmes ultimately unmasks a sophisticated revenge killer who forces victims to choose between placebo and poison. The reader is primed to be taken upon further medical adventures by Dr. Doyle but, after the first story, the trail goes cold.

As a physician in both private and (unsuccessful) specialty practice in both urban and rural England (as well as serving as ship's physician on global voyages and medic during the Second Anglo Boer War), Doyle has both the method and motive to infuse his stories with the latest in medical mystery and forensic techniques. In a time when society was undergoing rapid and fascinating technological changes, the stage was set; but, after his first Holmes story, the medical aspects of the stories become merely tangential. We can only deduce that the author's choices are intentional, for we know that Doyle based the character of Holmes, in part, on his medical school professor, Dr. Joseph Bell[1]. At Edinburgh, Bell was renowned for his ability to diagnose patients' disease and even discern their occupations solely upon his powers of observation. Doyle has Holmes use Bell's technique on many occasions, to the astonishment of Watson, the police and reader. Although the first official police forensics lab was not established until 1910 in France (Platt), Doyle still had exposure to the latest in forensic investigation: field trips to morgues and police inquiries guided by his professor, Dr. Henry Lightbrown, were part of the curriculum. There was abundant literature available, and by the time Doyle began his medical studies, Cristison's *Treatise on Poisons in Relation to Medical Jurisprudence* (1836), was already a classic.

Doyle chooses not to turn the Holmes stories into medical mysteries, perhaps to the consternation of Bell who had suggested some exciting cases for Doyle to consider. Doyle rejected these. In *Mr. Sherlock Holmes*, Bell expresses his frustration that Holmes's "surprising" techniques are commonplace in medicine:

> Sherlock Holmes' method is practiced by every good teacher of medicine or surgery every day … In medical diagnosis carried into ordinary life … you have Sherlock Holmes astonishing his somewhat dense friend Dr. Watson.

On an initial reading of the Canon, and perhaps thereafter, one expects there to be more medical science in Holmes stories. The late Victorian era was an exciting time of discovery and, although new advances were being made all the time, a physician's ability to *treat* disease lagged behind his ability to diagnose. Lister, for instance, was revolutionizing antiseptic surgery in Edinburgh while Doyle was there at medical school; the use of medical x-rays began in 1895; and the first criminal identification based on fingerprint evidence happened in 1892. Doctors could now tell a patient what was wrong but still had no cure. Perhaps it is this frustration that Doyle experiences firsthand that led him to create a detective who could rely on observation alone, while the police and medical men (as embodied by Watson) are left impotent. Reed asserts:

---

1   Strangely, for that matter, Doyle never has Holmes travel to his native Scotland.

It could be argued that there is an unspoken criticism of medical practice inherent in the adventures, accentuated by Watson as representative of the medical profession. One could imagine Doyle through the mouthpiece of Holmes scoffing at…the formulaic methods of his colleagues as compared with those of Bell.

Time and again we are presented with Watson's lack of critical thinking. In "The Priory School," when Holmes examines the dead German master next to a bicycle, Watson asks:

> "He could not have died of a skull fracture?"
> "In a morass, Watson?"
> "I am at a loss."

So much for Watson's forensic skills. In "The Dying Detective," Holmes, in disguise, feigns a non-existent tropical disease but Watson is unable to tell that the symptoms are a sham. Holmes excuses the doctor as "a practitioner of limited experience."

Doyle must have endured his own frustration with the limits of medical ability to solve even commonplace health issues. He watched helplessly as his father succumbed to the ravages of alcoholism, and his first wife died from the progressive consumption of tuberculosis. Here, perhaps, is where the character of Holmes becomes infused with Doyle's own experience: Holmes is addicted to cocaine, nicotine, and work. Like any addict, Holmes tells Watson that he can quit any time he likes: "Give me problems, give me work … and I can dispense with artificial stimulants." But Holmes's famous "three pipe problems" show us his dependence upon stimulants. There are allusions to Holmes having been cured but in "The Missing Three Quarter," Watson is "well aware that the fiend was not dead but sleeping."

Doyle himself was an auto-experimenter. Suffering from what today may be described as chronic trigeminal neuralgia debilitating facial nerve pain, Doyle took near toxic doses of tincture of gelsemium, documenting his findings and side effects[2] and, in one

---

2   Doyle's symptoms were moderate, however, high doses can cause paralysis and death. In 2012 the death of Chinese forestry tycoon Long Liyuan was linked to his ingesting a gelsemium-laced, slow-boiled cat stew.

of his only contributions to the medical literature, sending them to the *British Medical Journal*. Holmes is unafraid to do likewise, and Stamford warns Watson in *A Study in Scarlet* before meeting Holmes that he could "imagine his giving a friend a little pinch of the latest vegetable alkaloid, not out of malice … but out of a spirit of inquiry in order to have an accurate idea of the effects. I think he would take it himself with the same readiness."

That is just what happens in "The Devil's Foot." A Dr. Agar sends Holmes to the country to rest from exhaustion (and we wonder why *Watson* isn't treating Holmes) but Holmes ignores medical advice to investigate the strange doings at the Tregennis household where a woman has apparently died of fright, and her brothers driven mad by something they saw out the window. The family physician, Dr. Richards, has no clue and faints during examination of the victims. Watson concurs with Richards's diagnosis of fright causing the casualties but Holmes recognizes signs of poison and takes a sample of ashes from the fireplace. To prove his theory, Holmes burns the sample on a lamp nearly killing himself and Watson with the deadly fumes. We learn that another physician, Dr. Sterndale, has brought a sample of the Devil's Foot root poison from Africa which is so exotic that "European science would be powerless to detect it." One wonders why two doctors could not determine that something medical was afoot[3]?

Watson doesn't seem to learn by experience, and, in *The Sign of Four* he fails to recognize a similar case of alkaloid poisoning (poison dart) when he examines the body of Bartholomew Sholto frozen in a *rictus sardonicus*. Watson (who happens to have a stethoscope) examines Bartholomew's twin, Thaddeus, for a mitral valve disorder and declares him healthy. Doyle has given Watson the opportunity to at least engage in a differential diagnosis while one brother is suffering the psychological effects of mitral valve prolapse or possibly another nervous disorder while his twin is frozen in death. Surely Watson had to consider some type of congenital disorder when presented with twin patients. We

---

3   It *is* technically possible to die of fright: when terrorized, the body undergoes a "fight or flight" reaction which may cause a fatal cardiac event. It seems unlikely, though, that three people would undergo such severe, simultaneous consequences from a glance out the window.

can almost hear Dr. Bell screaming in the background—he, as all physicians who read the Holmes Canon, must be driven mad with frustration. It's not likely Watson fails to keep up with the medical literature—we often find him reading a medical journal or the latest surgical text; and, in "The Resident Patient," Watson is familiar with the publications of their client Dr. Percy Trevelyan's work on narcolepsy. Once more, it takes Holmes to elucidate that the medical experts are duped: Trevelyan is set up by Blessington, a man feigning illness and hiding from a cruel gang. His pursuer catches up with him and gains access to the premises disguised as a Russian nobleman pretending to suffer from catalepsy[4].

In *A Study in White*, Michael Lopez points out Doyle's use of doctors as criminals and the threat they pose. As doctors are supposed to be agents of good, the criminal doctor perpetuates a form of "treason" against patients and society. "The Speckled Band" is a good illustration. Doctor Grimesby Roylott, having returned from India where he served prison time for murdering his butler, terrorizes Surrey with his nastiness and collection of exotic animals. When one stepdaughter dies of mysterious causes, the other, Helen Stoner, becomes alarmed when Roylott makes her change bedrooms. Weird sounds in the night ensue and Holmes is called upon for help. Holmes surveys the strange scene, and suspects that Roylott wants to prevent his estate from passing to Helen upon her impending marriage. Holmes and Watson are able to stake out Helen's bedroom[5] and when a poisonous swamp adder descends through the ventilator Holmes is able to turn the snake back on its master.

Interestingly, in "The Speckled Band," Doyle mentions two other real-life evil doctors and tells Watson that "when a doctor

---

4   Doctors are easily fooled: in "The Man with the Twisted Lip," Watson is again confounded by Holmes disguised as a patient in need of rescue from the evils of the opium den. NB: Watson also seems to have no problem abandoning his patients at the drop of a hat when Holmes calls him—one wonders about the viability of Watson's medical practice.

5   Watson seems a bit scandalized sitting in a woman's bedroom at night, yet he has no problem making romantic advances on his client, Mary Morstan, in *The Sign of Four*—has the doctor crossed an ethical line?

goes bad he is the first of criminals." Holmes mentions Doctor E.W. Pritchard whose real life mirrors Roylott's. Like Roylott, Pritchard falls on hard financial times, and is suspected of murdering a servant. When his mother-in-law dies under suspicious circumstances and his wife falls ill, a colleague, Dr. Paterson, becomes suspicious but fails to blow the whistle. Only after his wife dies and an anonymous tip is sent to the police alerting them to poisoning (antimony) is Pritchard arrested. He is hanged in 1865. Roylott, however, is not brought to justice and Holmes admits to assisting in his demise (snake venom) but expresses no remorse in dispensing his own brand of redress. Holmes also mentions Dr. William Palmer, notorious womanizer and horse enthusiast, whose many relatives including a wife, uncle, and four children die (with insurance policies taken out on his wife and uncle); yet Palmer is not suspected of any malfeasance until his friend Cook falls ill and Palmer tries to claim Cook's gambling winnings. Exhumation of Palmer's victims reveals strychnine. Palmer is hanged in 1856[6].

With the success of Sherlock Holmes, Doyle was able to publish stories with medical themes and characters. In *Round the Red Lamp* (1894) the reading public gets a taste of medical realism that for some was an affront to their Victorian sensibilities. Still, these tales ranged from the humorous (a medical student fainting during his first operation) to the fantastic (a reanimated mummy chasing another doctor in training). Yet again, Doyle turns to the chilling possibilities of medicine and surgery gone awry and in two stories we see surgery used for the purposes of mutilation and revenge. In "Lady Sannox" a jealous husband dupes Doctor Stoner into disfiguring his wife (who was Stoner's lover)—here, a doctor operates on an anonymous, drugged woman: perhaps a symbol of the authoritarian attitudes of the physician, as well as being a cautionary tale about adultery. In a similar story published in *Pearson's Magazine* (1898), "The Retirement of Signor Lambert," Sir William Sparter is a tycoon who has everything he desires except the love of his beautiful young wife. When he suspects she is having

---

6   Palmer may have been the inspiration for Robert Norberton in "Shoscombe Old Place," in which Norberton conceals the death of his sister so that creditors will not foreclose until he has collected his winnings on a horse.

an affair with Lambert, a rising opera star, Sparter visits his local ENT and bones up on anatomy. He forces his wife to lure her lover to a rendezvous, where Sparter ambushes the singer, chloroforms him, and performs a grisly operation to sever his vocal cords. It is a shocking tale worthy of Poe, yet these striking medical stories seem out of place in the world of Sherlock Holmes where stories of blackmail, infidelity, and even murder take on a more genteel sensibility. Doyle, in his preface to *Red Lamp* prints a disclaimer:

> One cannot write of medical life and be merry over it. The stories, which while away a weary hour, fulfill an obviously good purpose, but no more so, I hold, than that which helps to emphasize the graver side of life. A tale which may startle the reader out of his usual grooves of thought and shocks him into seriousness plays into the part of the tonic in medicine, bitter to the taste, but bracing in the result.

Yet medical elements remain mostly absent in Sherlock Holmes—and the Holmes stories proved so successful that, time and again, Doyle is called upon, both by public and financial concerns, to continue the adventures of the detective (even after killing him at the Reichenbach Falls), taking Doyle away from what he considered the "serious" writings of historical fiction and spiritualism. When pressed by his mentor Dr. Bell to use medical themes to fictional advantage Doyle dismisses the suggestions as "not very practical."

In *A Study in Scarlet*, after we first meet Sherlock Holmes on the verge of a medico-forensic breakthrough, Doyle pulls the plug on the formula of a medical detective who relies little upon the lab and operates best by using pure observation and reason (Holmes never publishes his findings on a test for human hemoglobin, preferring to publish monographs on arcane topics such as identification of cigar ash, beekeeping, and the motets of Lassus). Doyle proved correct in that the reader would likely not enjoy being bogged down with medical details—and what we love in a Sherlock Holmes story is the satisfying experience of witnessing and being astonished by the process at work (even if Professor Bell laments that this is what any good doctor does every day). Watson becomes the reader's window into this engaging world. By having Watson reporting the cases, we can share his surprise and wonder in a way that does not work if Sherlock Holmes was merely writing his own memoirs.

In his latter days, Doyle rejected the tenets of his medical training and the cold rationalism of Holmes, and embraced spiritualism as both a bona fide phenomenon and as a gateway to a new religion. In an address to new medical students (1910) he, perhaps inappropriately, launches them on their scientific careers by expressing his doubts on the process:

> I had no great interest in the more recent developments of my profession and a very strong belief that much of the so-called progress was illusory.

He invites them to embrace the possibility of communicating with the dead.

In his varied writings Doyle saw the value in both "serious" as well as diversionary literature. In his final farewell to Holmes in *The Casebook* (1927), Doyle is dismissive of both Holmes and his readers while thanking them for supporting him so that he could write more important works (much as Holmes dismisses Watson in a paternal way):

> I have not found that these lighter sketches have prevented me from exploring … branches of literature (such) as history, poetry, historical novels, psychic research and drama. Had Holmes never existed I could not have done more, though he may perhaps have stood a little in the way of more serious literary work. And so reader, farewell to Sherlock Holmes! I thank you for your constancy and can but hope that some return has been made in the shape of that distraction of the worries of life and stimulating change of thoughts, which can only be found in the fairy kingdom of romance.

The magic of Sherlock Holmes is that once his methods are made clear, we fantasize that we could master his techniques ourselves, all the while knowing that while we are hoping to participate on some level, like Watson, we will never acquire these abilities. As Holmes gently informs Watson in *The Hound of the Baskervilles*:

> It may be that you are not yourself luminous, but you are a conductor of light.

And so, while as readers, we may have the expectation or perception that Sherlock Holmes would be a champion of contemporary medical science, Doyle's stories actually highlight the limitations and dangers of medicine. Even the literature written about Sherlock Holmes and medicine seems to overlook this fact and just assumes that the science is there. Guthrie, for instance, in *Sherlock Holmes in Medicine*, concludes that there is a "kinship" between Sherlock Holmes/detectives and physicians but pays little attention to the way that medicine is portrayed in the stories and concludes that the stories are "dated." Today, leading forensic pathologists are referred to as "modern Sherlock Holmes's"—and perhaps they *are* in the sense that they are able to make keen observations and synthesize a variety of data to tell a plausible story from a dead body and related clues; but they *do* bring all possible science to bear upon their investigations. One of these people is Professor Keith Simpson of England. In his book *Sherlock Holmes on Medicine and Science* (1983) his "chapter" on Watson's contributions is less than three pages! He criticizes Doyle for Watson's anatomical blunder in "Shoscombe Old Place" wherein Watson misidentifies a charred bone fragment. He also takes Doyle to task that Sherlock Holmes never has to appear in court to give forensic testimony. Simpson misses the point—Doyle did not care if his medical information was accurate: the medical facts are often secondary trivialities for the reader of a Holmes adventure.

When I began writing Sherlock Holmes stories I am sure that I must have felt sorry for Watson and apologetic that Doyle did not seize upon the exciting discoveries happening in medicine at the turn of the twentieth century. I felt a need to infuse my stories with bits of medical history and highlight Watson's potential to contribute to an investigation using his medical insight[7].

Perhaps Simpson is expressing the modern view that today we could not imagine a detective failing to make use of all the forensic/medical science available. Television has done well to embrace this desire (there are seven CSI and NCIS shows) and we can go back to *Quincy* of the 1970s and *House, MD* of the 2000s where a Sherlock and Watson team are all portrayed as medical professionals. While *Quincy* may be campy, he does, like Holmes, spend a

7   See "Watson's Wound," *SHMM*, Vol. 3, "A House Gone Mad," *SHMM*, Vol. 7, "Blackheath Collapse," *SHMM*, Vol. 9.

lot of time demonstrating to the police how erroneous their conclusions can be when they do not scrutinize the evidence. Meanwhile, House embraces his own addictions: drugs and diagnostics. He reiterates the medical dictum that "symptoms do not lie" but to get at the truth of a diagnostic problem he has little regard as to how much hell he will put his team or patient through. To House, like the readers of the Canon, the *game/process* is what matters. More recently the BBC's *Sherlock* finds the detective using both the lab and the smartphone to extreme advantage. In some way it feels right that Sherlock embraces the latest technology in this modern adaptation. In *Elementary*, after a case with a bad outcome, Watson withdraws from practice likely due to psychological pressures. We are reminded that in spite of the best intentions, medical science has its limits. While House would accept this, stating, "It is the nature of medicine that you are going to screw up and kill someone," the modern Watson cannot. Lucy Liu's character, like the original Watson, contributes little of her medical experience to investigations and the writers have channeled Doyle's medical misgivings—interestingly, Watson of *Elementary* is never introduced as *doctor*: she is only referred to as *Joan* or *Ms.* Watson, emphasizing the failures of medical science and the concept of the ineffective physician.

Holmes famously points out that, "You see but you do not observe." In terms of the medical and scientific content of Sherlock Holmes, perhaps readers, writers and researchers have all been guilty of seeing something in the stories that is not only *not* there, but failing to notice what Dr. Arthur Conan Doyle left us to observe in plain sight.

BIBLIOGRAPHY

Bell, Joseph, "Mr. Sherlock Holmes," *The Illustrated Sherlock Holmes Treasury*, NY: Avenel, 1986 (originally published in *The Bookman* 1892).

Billings, Harold, "Materia Medica of Sherlock Holmes," *Baker Street Journal* 2006: 37-46.

Conan Doyle, Arthur, "The Retirement of Signor Lambert," *Pearson's Magazine*, Dec.1898.

Conan Doyle, Arthur, *Memoirs and Adventures*, London: Hodder and Staunton, 1924.

Conan Doyle, Arthur, *Round the Red Lamp Being Facts and Fancies of Medical Life*, London: Methuen, 1894.

Conan Doyle, Arthur, *The Complete Sherlock Holmes*, NY: Barnes & Noble, 1992.

Conan Doyle, Arthur, with Robert Darby, "The Romance of Medicine," in *Round the Red Lamp and Other Medical Writing*, NY: Valancourt, 2007 (Originally in *St. Mary's Hospital Gazette* Vol. 16, 1910).

Conan Doyle, Arthur, "Gelsemium as a Poison," (Letter) *British Medical Journal*, Sept., 9, 1879.

Cristison, Robert, *A Treatise on Poisons in Relation to Medical Jurisprudence*, Edinburgh: Adam and Charles Black, 1836.

Devein, Hannah, "Gelsemium: the Plant That Can Cause Paralysis," *The Guardian*, May 18, 2015.

Guthrie, Douglas, "Sherlock Holmes and Medicine," *Canad. Med. J.* Oct 25, 1961: (85) 996-1000.

Harrison, Michael, ed., *Beyond Baker Street: A Sherlockian Anthology*, NY: Bobbs-Merrill,1976.

Larner, Andrew, "Sherlock Holmes and Neurology," *Advances Clin. Neuroscience and Rehab*. March 2011: 21-22.

Lopez, Michael, "A Study in White: Medicine and Crime According to Sherlock Holmes," *Linguae.it*, 2011:33-42.

Lycett, Andrew, *The Man Who Created Sherlock Holmes*, NY: Free Press, 2007.

Platt, Marvin and Russell Fisher, *History of Forensic Pathology*, Springfield: Charles Thomas, 1993.

Reed, James "A Medical Perspective on the Adventures of Sherlock Holmes," *Med. Humanities* 2001: (27) 76-81.

Retchin, Sheldon, "Does Giving a Diagnosis of MVP Cause a Patient to Develop Symptoms and Functional Disabilities," *Robert Wood Johnson Foundation* Jan 24, 2013.

Shaw, Albert ed., (Review of *Round the Red Lamp*), *Review of Reviews*, NY: Dec. 1894.

Simpson, Keith, *Sherlock Holmes on Medicine and Science*, NY: Magico Magazine, 1983.

The Sociéte Sherlock Holmes's *Conan Doyle Encyclopedia* was also consulted: www.sshf.com/encyclopedia.

Dr. Kilstein writes from Rhode Island. His novel *Wise Men* was published 2013 and *Destroying Angel: A Novel of Surgery and Witchcraft* was recently re-issued in ebook format.

THE BUTTERFLY AND THE SPIDER

by Stan Trybulski

The man held the tiny creature in the sink and let the tap water gently run over its wings and body. How exquisite is this *papillon* with its frail beauty, he thought, glad that only moments ago he had extricated it from the silken clutches of the spider web that had formed on his terrace.

Even spiders must eat, the man realized. But not this day and not this little beauty. He carried the *papillon* back onto the terrace and set it on the cushion of the chaise longue and watched as it tried to flap its red and gold wings. Even after the washing, he could see that it was struggling, one of its four wings crooked at an awkward angle, trapped by the gossamer chains that had ensnared it. He left it there lying in the sun while he went back inside. He shaved, dressed and finished his *espresso* while looking out at the water of the *calanque*, the tiny cove outside the city. He looked at his watch; he would have loved another cup of the strong coffee but there was no time. He had a job to do and like the spider he must also eat. He would have his coffee and check the *papillon* on his return.

✗   ✗   ✗   ✗

The drive into Marseille along the corniche was magnificent. The fall sun was bright. The wind coming across the Mediterranean was kicking up white caps that crested over sparkling blue waves. Each winding curve of the narrow road gave him a different view of the rocks and sea. After he had done his work, he would drive back the same way. When he reached the long beach he saw few people on the sand and no one was swimming in the water, turned brown by the churning, wind-driven waves. Past the beach, the traffic began to grow and he turned his attention back to the road.

In the city, the man parked the car in the underground municipal garage behind the Hotel de Ville and walked up the streets of the hilly Panier until he came to a building near the top. Inside the dimly lit hallway was a row of five mailboxes. He withdrew a small shiny key from his trousers pocket and unlocked the mailbox on the end. He took out a package and looking around to make sure that no was watching, he opened it, already knowing what was inside, but not knowing the manufacturer.

He was pleased by what he found: a small caliber Danish match pistol with a ten-shot magazine. Perfect for business on a crowded street; he would not have to be up close for the kill shots and the noise would be minimal. He slapped the magazine into the butt of the handle and pulled out his shirt so it hung over his trousers and then tucked the gun under his belt at the side of his hip.

He relocked the mailbox and walked back down the steep hill of the Panier and along the perimeter of the Vieux Port and its crowded fresh fish market. When he reached the other side of the harbor, he turned and walked inland. Near the Rue Paradis he found the address he was looking for and walked past it. It was a small restaurant patronized by business people at noontime but it was now approaching three p.m. and he knew that it would be almost deserted.

He walked past the place again and then turned back and went inside. He quickly spotted the man he was supposed to see; a bald man sitting at table in a corner, drinking a cup of coffee. The bald man was talking to another man at the table, his hands talking along with him in the Mediterranean fashion.

The man with the Danish match pistol walked back outside, put on a pair of surgical gloves and waited. About fifteen minutes later a dark Mercedes pulled up in front of the restaurant and the driver went inside. He returned and opened the rear passenger door, holding it for the bald man. The man with the match pistol walked rapidly toward the car, taking out the pistol without breaking his stride. Something about his movement must have attracted the bald man's attention for he looked at him and the pistol and started to duck into the car.

Two shots, hardly the popping sound of a balloon and the bald man fell into the gutter. The driver reached inside his coat pocket but never even had a chance to grip the weapon holstered there as three rounds ripped into his chest. The shooter tossed the match pistol under the Mercedes and quickly walked away. He took a circuitous route back to the parking garage, along the way dropping the surgical gloves down a storm drain.

On the return drive along the corniche, he stopped at a restaurant that overlooked the Mediterranean. He sat at a table by the window and ordered a sea bream and a half-bottle of Cassis rosé. While his food was being prepared, he sipped the wine and looked out at the sea. It always calmed him after a hard day's work. When the meal came he ate slowly, savoring the chunks of fish which had been prepared in a spicy fish stew. A working man must always devote some time for life's little pleasures, he told himself.

Afterwards, he drove slowly along the corniche road and then turned inland for the long treacherous climb up and down the steep hills back to the *calanque*. At the end of the narrow cove, he parked his car and climbed along the rocky path to his cottage. Changing into his bathing suit, he went out on the terrace to check on the *papillon*. The butterfly was gone and he did not know whether to be happy or sad for while it had clearly regained its freedom, he would miss its beauty.

He walked over to the edge of the terrace and climbed out onto the rocky ledge. Unlike the roiling sea along the beaches, the water here in the narrow *calanque* was protected by high rocky cliffs and was so clear he could see underneath the surface all the way to where the rocky ledge dropped off into an abyss. He knew the water would be as cool and clean as the tap water he had washed the *papillon* with. He also knew that a long hard swim in its coldness would wash away the bonds that imprisoned his soul. At least for the time being, anyway. And in his line of business, the time being was all there really was.

Later, as he toweled himself off, he saw that another spider web had formed in the corner of the terrace but the man did not destroy this one. For while in his heart he would always admire the fragile beauty of the *papillon*, the butterfly; in his mind he understood well the brutal necessity of the spider.

✗

Stan Trybulski, who wrote *One Trick Pony* and other crime novels, was a Brooklyn felony trial prosecutor before he went into private practice. Before he entered the legal profession, he was a newspaper reporter, college administrator, and bartender (not all at the same time). He now divides his time between France and "two acres of Connecticut tranquility."

VOICES

by Michael Haynes

I knew I wanted the house as soon as we pulled into its driveway. Everything that the agent had told us looked to be true, and as we climbed up the hill to the porch I was hoping the inside would be as wonderful as the outside and that my husband would love it as much as I did.

The agent guided us through the house. We started in the entryway painted in my favorite shade of pale blue and ended in the upstairs library. The library was wonderful, with more than enough bookshelves for all of our books, and an enormous window overlooking the ocean.

After our last son graduated from college, we decided to leave the suburban neighborhood we lived in since our wedding and find an isolated house with a view. We looked at several since that decision, and Paul was scrutinizing each room in this house as he had in all the others. Most of those houses would have been acceptable to me, but he had found something wrong with each of them. As he looked over each corner, I started to wonder what he would find wrong with this one, what little detail would keep us away from it and its seaside view.

The agent finished his talk and waited as we stood there, Paul still looking over the library while I watched the tide come in.

"What do you think?" I asked Paul, nervous, but ready to fight to live there.

"Do you like it?" he asked me.

"It's everything I want."

He nodded, thought for a moment, and told the agent to draw up the papers.

✗　✗　✗　✗

We moved in two months later. Furniture, placed randomly, filled our new living room, and every other room and hall had one or more stacks of boxes with markings to remind us of the contents. After several hours of unpacking and many minutes of wandering through our new home, we went out to walk down the oceanside path we could see from our library.

The sun was low in the west, not yet on the horizon, but in that state of change where it evolves from a compact and blindingly harsh yellow to a diffuse orange-red. The ocean lapped at the sand and birds flew overhead while we sat at the edge of the trail. I would spend several moments looking out to sea, then turn to see our new house from a different perspective. They were both beautiful, and I knew that I was where I was supposed to be, where I should always have been.

While I was thinking this, Paul took my hand and gently squeezed it. He didn't say anything, he just held my hand and looked around. I glanced over at his face and thought for a moment that he felt the same way that I did about the house and the trail and the sea. It wasn't like him to be that way. I was used to him being practical.

"A house is a house," he'd said when we chose our first one, "all that matters is that it's well built." The years had changed him, but I couldn't be sure that the wistful look on his face represented his pleasure at the beauty of it all. For all I knew, he might have been thinking about how much more money it would cost us to keep up a larger house and drive farther to the city.

"You're sure you like it?" I asked him after a moment.

He paused, staring out at the ocean, then he looked over to the house before he answered. "I do."

✗   ✗   ✗   ✗

That night was the first time we heard them. We were lying in our bed, the only furnishing in the room. Paul was asleep, and I was reading a book and occasionally glancing out the window at the moon's broken reflection in the ocean.

The voice was Emily's, but I didn't know that at the time. All I heard was a soft whistle, perhaps the sound of the wind blowing through some trees nearby or in a small open space somewhere in the house. The sound was soothing when I started listening, and then I began to hear words. At first I thought my imagination was responsible, but the more I listened, the more I was sure that someone was speaking. Curious then, I set my book on the bed to listen more carefully.

"… a long time ago and I remember how it felt and smelled and everything," said the whistle, the words fading in and out. By then I was sitting up in bed, straining, trying to make sense out of the words I heard. The voice was just quiet enough that I couldn't quite understand it, but loud enough that when I tried to go back to my book it distracted me.

"I wanted to wear it everywhere," the silky voice said, "even just out to the store. Of course I couldn't …" And then I couldn't hear the rest.

Frustrated, I wandered to the window, expecting to see a few girls sitting below us, talking to each other. I looked out and saw no one, only the moon, trees, and ocean. The voice continued, a soft whisper that I couldn't understand. I paced the bedroom, looking for a radio left behind by the previous owners. Something. But I couldn't find anything to explain the sounds I heard.

As I kept searching for the voice's origin, I looked around the room even more cautiously. Even though there was nothing to hide behind, I began expecting someone—or something—to jump out from somewhere at any time. I nudged Paul awake and asked him to listen.

He sat up, still slightly asleep, and listened for a moment, the night silent except for the wordless voice.

"Do you hear it?" I asked him.

"I hear a whistling sound, the wind maybe," he muttered.

"No. It's a voice. I heard it talking. Keep listening."

Several minutes passed and the soft whistle stayed wordless. Had I just dreamed hearing a voice talking, and woken Paul for nothing?

Then from the whistle, "And to top it all off, he stood me up. I got to wear it for my little brother and my mom. Now isn't that a story?"

The whistle stopped then. Silence filled the room where those last soft words had pushed it out seconds before.

Paul didn't say anything, he just looked around the room.

"Did you hear it?"

"Yes."

I opened my mouth to ask another question.

"No," he said, "I don't know what it is."

Paul got up and paced for a while, then came back to bed and fell asleep. I couldn't relax enough to sleep much that night, listening for a distant whisper. Once I thought I might have heard it again, but it was gone before I could be sure. Sometime that night, I fell asleep.

✗   ✗   ✗   ✗

The next day I woke up hoping to hear a voice, but only heard silence.

Several days later, while Paul was away at work, I heard the whisper again. This time I heard several voices.

I heard the speaker from the night before first; she was talking about growing up on a farm with her two older brothers. It was still hard to understand a lot of what she said, but her words seemed clearer. When she finished her story, another lady, Christine, told a story about living in inner-city Boston.

Christine was easier to understand than Emily, and her words crackled with reality. The boy down the street who was her best friend, the fruit shop on the corner, her mother baking a roast all day while she and her friends played upstairs and could smell it slowly cooking; all were as real to me as if I had been there, living my own life as they happened.

As I listened, not thinking about anything except their stories, I thought I saw something move from the corner of my eye. I turned to look at it, but nothing was there. After glancing around the room, I went back to listening to Christine, but her voice was fainter and she was ending her story.

"…Then we moved out here, and I never saw any of them again. Oh, we wrote a couple of letters, but never anything much. So that's my story." The talking stopped. In the silence that followed I thought about what was happening. I knew what my first, instinctive, reaction was, but for all I considered possible, ghosts had never been part of my world. I tried hard to think of some other explanation, but none of them seemed very rational, either.

I tried to push the mystery of it out of my mind, and thought instead about their stories. I heard a storyteller once when I was young; he had been travelling for years just telling stories and their stories were like his. They were so rich and colorful, you could feel yourself inside them, and they almost seemed alive. I wanted to hear the voices speak again, just as I had wanted the storyteller not to leave our library and go somewhere else to tell other children stories.

The silence continued while I put silverware in drawers and clothes in closets. I listened carefully for a wispy whistle all day while I unpacked, hoping to hear another story.

⚡   ⚡   ⚡   ⚡

The next few days we heard the voices often. Sometimes it was just me listening, sometimes just Paul, and lots of times both of us were there. I talked about calling the agent, asking him about all of this, and Paul even talked briefly about moving somewhere else to get away from the voices, but neither of us took those ideas very seriously. Maybe Paul was softening a bit, I thought during these days. I couldn't imagine the old Paul living in a house with mysterious voices, let alone spending hours listening to them.

The third day I tried talking to one of the voices. A man named Peter, who was Emily's older brother, was talking about the people he spent time with during his college years.

"Hello?" I cut in impulsively as he talked.

Peter stopped talking, paused for a moment, then picked his story back up. I called out again, without even thinking about what I was doing, and Peter stopped talking once more. I was reminded of the way that someone who was talking might stop for a second to try to listen for something that they thought they heard.

I tried to say more, wanting some other kind of answer, but it was clear that Peter couldn't understand me. I started to wonder if they even knew we were here, listening to everything they said to each other.

When I asked Paul, he said that he thought they had no idea, but I wasn't sure. I asked him why we sometimes heard only one person talking if they weren't talking to us. He thought about that for a moment before saying that we were probably hearing them talk to someone else who wasn't saying anything. I told him that I thought he was just rationalizing, but he held by his explanation firmly and I left it at that.

⚡   ⚡   ⚡   ⚡

It wasn't until several days later that we found out they knew we existed. We had finally gotten somewhere close to settled in, our things unpacked and in some semblance of order. The voices were much louder than they had been the first night. It was like listening in on a conversation happening just five feet away, maybe on the other side of a wall through an open door; we could hear them but not see them. Several times I thought I had half-seen someone standing near me while I listened to the voices, but every time I looked nothing was there.

We were sure they knew about us, and finally saw one of them clearly the day Paul was setting up his workshop in the basement. He was carrying things up and down the steps and listening to Isaac talk about when his first son was born. While he was carrying a box of tools down, he started to lose his balance. He tried to straighten himself, then tried to put the tools down on a step. He didn't notice Isaac's voice had stopped.

He heard Isaac yell, "Watch out!" as he continued to fight to regain his balance. Then, from the middle of the air in front of him, two hands formed and pushed him back gently, helping him stay upright.

The hands faded, and a middle-aged man appeared in the air two steps down from Paul. Paul stepped back and paused for a moment.

"Thanks," he said, startled and not sure what to do or say.

Isaac shrugged. "You needed some help."

"Still, thanks, I appreciate it." Paul reached out to shake Isaac's hand without thinking. At first, his hand just waved through the area where he saw Isaac's hand, then Isaac faded but his hand became more solid and Paul shook it.

As this was happening, I arrived at the top of the steps. I had heard Paul cry out and ran through the house, afraid of what I would see. When I got there, Paul was standing, and my racing heartbeat slowed as thoughts of heart attacks and strokes slid aside. Then I saw Isaac standing in front of him and watched them shake hands. My heart sped up again and I stayed there, amazed and a bit afraid.

I watched while Paul carried the tools down the steps then stopped to ask some questions. I slipped off as they talked, feeling vaguely guilty for watching.

I went back to the living room, and he came upstairs to tell me what had happened. For some reason, I felt a bit of a chill when he told me that the only thing specific Isaac said to him was, "We want you to hear our stories."

Something about that put me on edge and I almost mentioned it to Paul, but decided not to. I had no idea what it meant and didn't feel like defending a feeling against Paul's logical scrutiny.

✗   ✗   ✗   ✗

By the time we heard the voices again, I had dismissed the memory of the chill and the nervous feeling Isaac's words had brought.

In the next week, we saw most of the other inhabitants of our house. There were eight, and they had all lived here at some time in their life. Several had died in it or near it, while the others had gone somewhere else to live and die. Seeing eight other people occasionally walking through my house was disconcerting at first, but no more so than the voices had been. Their stories were still magical enough that I couldn't feel as if they were intruding on our time. Many times I even stopped what I was doing to sit down and listen.

Paul and I hadn't bothered to hook up the television. At night we would sit on the living room couch and rest, hoping to hear some of them talk. Their stories were more interesting than most shows, anyway, and as Paul jokingly reminded me, there were no commercials.

One night all of them suddenly showed up. As we sat on the couch they appeared, sitting in a semi-circle in front of us. Peter told us a story first, about the first girl he ever truly loved. Then Amy talked about the day her father died. Emily told us about the work she did on her parents' farm every morning before school.

Each one of them told a story and every story was real and alive. Some of the stories were sad, like Amy's, but others were fun and exciting, remembrances of Christmases, birthdays, and Fourth of Julys past. It felt even more as if I was living through the events they told me about now.

The phone rang during Peter's second story. I didn't want to get up to answer it and neither did Paul. We heard the answering machine running in the background, but didn't listen to hear who was leaving a message. I figured that if it was really important, they'd call back and that time I would answer it.

The next morning they were still talking. Someone knocked on our door, but we didn't answer it. The phone rang several other times, but I went against my previous decision and ignored it.

All we did was listen to their stories. They had hundreds of years of life to tell us about and never had any difficulty thinking of something new. We talked to them several times during those days, but neither of us had much to say and we went back to just sitting, quietly listening.

⚹ ⚹ ⚹ ⚹

Time passed. Neither Paul nor I went anywhere, choosing only to sit and listen. I don't really know how long we had been there when Isaac stopped in the middle of a story. He walked over to where we sat and embraced us. He was much clearer and more solid than I remembered seeing any of them before.

"Stand up, now," he said.

Both of us stood up, first Paul and then me. Something felt different, something that I couldn't figure out. I looked around the room. Everything seemed right, but it didn't feel right. I looked over at Paul, and he looked like he always did. Something had changed, I was sure, but the change was as intangible as the whisper we heard the first night in our bedroom.

"We want to hear you tell your stories," Isaac said to us. I felt that same chill that I had felt when Paul told me what Isaac said on the stairs. I think that, at that moment, Paul understood all of it, but I was still trying to think it through.

"We're not alive anymore, are we?" Paul asked suddenly.

Isaac shook his head. "No, but not any more or less alive than we are." He waved his hand to indicate all the other people there.

When Isaac shook his head, my fists clenched. For a moment I wanted to jump on him and hit him as hard as I could for what they had done to us. I almost laughed hysterically when I wondered if I even could hit him. I stopped myself then, waiting to see what Paul would do.

He nodded as if it was the answer he expected. He looked around the room for a minute, wistfully, then carefully sat down where he had before. He was much calmer than I expected him to be and his calmness affected me. We were dead, I thought, but so were they and they had managed to seem alive to us for these last few weeks. Paul waved to me, and after a few seconds I sat down next to him as he started to talk.

"I met Mary, my wife, when we were both in college …" he began, telling them about our first date, the night he proposed to me, and our wedding. The first few minutes I was still tense, trying to understand my new situation, then I relaxed and just listened. I knew everything that would happen, I had literally lived it, but still it captivated me. It was as if another voice had been added to the eight I had been hearing before, and it was wonderful.

So now we are part of the voices. I hope you can hear us.

That is my story. Won't you tell us yours?

Michael Haynes lives in Central Ohio. An ardent short story reader and writer, Michael has had stories appear in venues such as *Ellery Queen's Mystery Magazine*, *Beneath Ceaseless Skies*, and *Nature*. Chair of the Cinevent Classic Film Convention, he also enjoys geocaching and live music. His website is http://michaelhaynes.info.

INCIDENT AT PUERTO ANGEL

by Dianne Neral Ell

Tuesday, September 23

In days to come, Philip Gordon would wonder why he hadn't paid attention to the warning signs. They were there. But he tended to attribute the recent oddities in his friend Charles Sheridan's behavior to either his job as president of SGS Industries or the ongoing alimony battles with his former wife. It never occurred to Phil Gordon that there was something deeper bothering 'Chummy' as his friends called him—not until that late September morning when Gordon arrived at his Wall Street office.

Carter Gordon and Partners, a Wall Street investment firm, had a system that warned of irregularities in client accounts. When a problem occurred that was outside the parameters of ordinary business, it triggered an alarm that blinked a red light even when the computer was off.

Gordon, who had just walked into his office at nine thirty a.m. after a client meeting at the Downtown Club, put his container of coffee from the first floor deli on his desk and stared at the blinking light. He turned the computer on and within ten seconds it opened to the warning page. It was Chummy Sheridan's SGS Industries Investment Account. The message said: *per your wire instructions, twenty million dollars has been released from SGS Industries account, Savoy Bank of London, England, to New York Bank, NY.*

Gordon sunk into his soft leather high backed chair and stared at the screen in disbelief. His eyes hung on the word "*your*," meaning Carter Gordon. Except he was the only one who could release that amount of money, and he wasn't in the office yesterday to sign for it. He frantically tapped a few keys that would give him more information. All he saw was the release time of the funds from the Savoy Bank. No information as to who authorized the wire transfer. He immediately called Nigel Green at the Savoy.

"Good Lord, Gordon. I only found out a few minutes ago about the SGS wire transfer," Nigel said in his high British accent. "What's your friend Chummy need with twenty million? Buying a third world country, a yacht, covering gambling debts? Any idea why he'd have to sneak around to remove that money from the account? I know you didn't authorize it because I have a copy of the wire transfer in front of me. To the untrained eye, the proper authorizations, yours and Walt Sutton's, are there. But I know they're not your signatures. Unfortunately, our wire transfer department thought they were. So they went ahead and released the funds."

Gordon continued to search his laptop for data that wasn't available. "I have nothing on this end authorizing the transfer. Can you fax me a copy? I'd like to see it before I talk to Robin Glasser, our person in charge of these things."

"Sending it now by regular fax," Nigel said. "Not to gnaw at your back, but I thought your company had safeguards to prevent this type of thing from happening."

Gordon waited in silence until he heard the ring and saw the two sheets of paper appear on the fax tray. The wire transfer had two signatures as required. His and Walt Sutton, Carter Gordon's finance VP. Nigel was right. The signatures were a forgery … but a good one.

"Like you said, not our signatures."

"You weren't in, I wasn't in either. So who from your company would know our movements and how to time the transfer without anyone discovering the theft? We need answers, you know, and quickly, before our bank audit starts next week."

"Only one person," Gordon said, "Robin Glasser. But she could not have done this on her own. I'll find out what's going on and while I do that, keep an eye on the funds."

Gordon hung up and looked at the SGS account. He wondered what else Chummy might have been up to. His friend's lifestyle since the divorce from his second wife tended to make the social columns. Among the women he dated was Robin Glasser—the tall, attractive movie-star-looking brunette who kept the administrative end of Carter Gordon, including wire transfers, running smoothly. And who was now neck deep in fraud. He had also taken up with Madison Hall. Blond. Model-type looks. Former FBI agent who, along with her brother, owned an investigative agency that also handled freelance mercenary work.

As he thought about Robin, he pressed the number for her extension. She didn't answer. It was already past ten. She should have been in. If nothing else, Robin had been punctual over the months she had worked at Carter Gordon. He phoned the personnel department. They hadn't heard from her. He already knew Walt Sutton's signature was forged, so there was no sense alerting him to the theft. He'd find out soon enough.

Next, he punched in Chummy Sheridan's number. Gordon's temper was rising by the moment. He was told Chummy was in a meeting. "Get him out. It's urgent."

"Boring meeting," Sheridan said when he got on the call. "What do you need?"

"Twenty million. How did you get Robin Glasser to forge a wire transfer taking those funds out of your business investment account?"

There was silence for a moment.

"I didn't. What are you talking about?"

His surprise seemed genuine. But Gordon's gut told him differently. "Twenty million of your money is on the move from Nigel's bank to New York. Why didn't you just tell me you needed it? Now it looks like theft, fraud, or any other way you want to describe what took place."

"Holy crap."

Gordon could hear his heavy breathing. Chummy knew about the money.

"Has it gotten to New York yet?"

"No," Gordon said. "Probably not for another two hours. We can't intercept at this point."

"I don't believe it. I really don't believe it. Let me call you back."

The next person Gordon needed to talk to was Jason Moore, a fraud investigator. Jason had contacts and sources that even the CIA would envy. He quickly told his long-time friend what was happening.

"I'll get on it immediately," Jason said. "I wonder what twenty million buys these days. I'll find something, don't worry. In the meantime, keep an eye on the money and find Robin Glasser. Even if you have to go to her apartment."

✗ ✗ ✗ ✗

With other client matters to attend to, it was a little past three o'clock when Gordon got off the subway at the 72nd Street station and walked south for two blocks to 70th, where Robin lived. The red-brick apartment building was halfway down the tree-lined street. The lobby was busy. Gordon paused, looked for the doorman and, not seeing him, strode directly across the lobby and took the elevator to the fifth floor. It was a long hallway and apartment "G" was at the end of it.

He knocked. No one answered. He tried the knob. It turned and the door swung open. Except for a sofa and a table, the room was empty. He called Robin's name but she didn't answer. A suitcase stood by the doorway into the bedroom. He walked in and found her on the floor face up. The bullet hole in her forehead stopped her from telling him about the twenty million.

What was so important that she had to die? He thought of Chummy. Had he killed Robin? Careful not to leave any prints, he quickly went through the apartment, which had been cleaned out. He opened the suitcase. Summer-type clothes. Tucked into a zippered compartment was boarding information about a flight to Acapulco leaving at three p.m. She would have been gone by one, making her death sometime this morning. Whoever killed her removed anything relating to the twenty million dollars. That included her cell phone and laptop, if she had one.

Gordon stepped into the hall, closing the door behind him. He thought of calling his friend from the twentieth precinct to report Robin's murder, then decided against it. In five minutes he was outside hailing a cab to take him to Chummy's Fifth Avenue apartment. His friend had not called back. When he reached the building, the doorman was only too happy to tell him that Mr. Sheridan left around three with a suitcase. Dressed casually. And saying he'd be gone for a week to Mexico.

Chummy could have killed her. There was time. Gordon walked out into the late afternoon September sunlight and thought about his next step. He had nothing. Not Robin. Not Chummy. And no idea about why the twenty million was needed.

Then he got the call from Nigel. "The money is on the move. It's come into New York and shortly will be heading out again. This time to California Consolidated of L.A."

"Francis Osborne." Gordon stared at the cracks in the sidewalk. "Didn't see that coming."

"Are Osborne and Chummy friends?" Nigel asked.

"Yes. By the way, Chummy's left town. Stopped by his apartment building. Maybe he's visiting Osborne. I'll head there. Let you know what I find."

On his cell phone he found a text from Chummy. "*Don't have an answer for you. Going to find one.*" It was sent at 2:30 p.m.

Wednesday, September 24

Francis Osborne came out of the military straight into the Celtics. From there he crossed the country to the Lakers. And somewhere along the way he learned enough about banking to get hired by California Consolidated. It may have been a public relations move at first, but now Osborne was president. He was doing well for himself and the bank, especially as he paddled treacherous international waters. So why get involved with the twenty million which had nefarious underpinnings?

Gordon sat in his hotel room at the Biltmore across the street from California Consolidated. He planned to drop in on Osborne around ten a.m. Before then he had Jason run a quick check on Osborne. The only oddity that came out of it was a meeting that took place between the banker and a man named Tom Sherwood. Perhaps it was nothing: former Laker meets with former sports promoter. Or … why would the president of an international bank have lunch with a troubleshooter/dirty trickster who worked for Michael Springer, the vice president of the United States?

"Maybe Osborne's looking for a Presidential post if Springer goes into the White House," Jason suggested. "Except my gut tells me that's not the case. It's hard to connect this meeting to the twenty million, but that may be what we have to do."

"When did this meeting take place?"

"Yesterday. Lunch time."

"This involves Chummy. I'm sure he knows Sherwood."

"I'll keep digging," Jason said. "Keep in touch."

✗ ✗ ✗ ✗

Phil Gordon never made it to his meeting with Francis Osborne. As he headed down the hall to the elevator, a call came in from Nigel telling him that the money was now heading to Banco de Mexico in Mexico City.

"Chummy was surprised by the theft," Gordon said to Nigel. "My guess … someone else working with Robin Glasser started the ball rolling. Chummy knew who and panicked. He was able to change the wire transfer orders and the money's direction. Since we don't know what's going down it could spell problems for Osborne."

"True. I hope Francis doesn't end up being a loose end. It might be bad for his health. Anyway, talk to the bank manager in Mexico City. His name is Marco Harris. Good man. Mention my name."

It was now going on ten. Gordon decided to have a good cup of coffee. In the meantime, he'd think about meeting with Osborne. He got off the elevator and headed for Gallery Café. As he entered the lobby with its vaulted ceiling and marble floor, he saw who he thought was Tom Sherwood walk in and take a table near some potted palms. He got his phone out and snapped a photo. Not five minutes later Francis Osborne joined him.

Gordon watched. If he sat down with them, that would stunt the conversation and he'd never learn why they were meeting. There might be another way. He looked around for the waiter he met last night. Saw him getting ready to carry water to the tables. Gordon pulled some money out of his wallet and went up to him.

"A small favor, Alex," he said to the short, heavy-set man with dark eyes and graying hair. He pointed to Osborne's table. "I need to know what they're talking about. If, by chance, you happen to overhear something."

The waiter smiled. "With pleasure. Mr. Osborne treats the staff here like trash."

The meeting lasted one cup of coffee. By the time Gordon walked the length and back of the huge lobby, they were gone. He sat down at a table. Alex came over.

"The other man was angry with Osborne," Alex said. "He said something about the money not being where it should be. If

Gordon didn't have it by evening …" He made a motion of a throat being cut.

He gave Alex an additional fifty, telling him it was for his children, then he went upstairs to pack. He learned more through the waiter than he would from Osborne. Time to go to Mexico City.

✗   ✗   ✗   ✗

The flight landed at six thirty. Gordon went directly to the Meridian Hotel near the bank. Later, as he sat at the crowded bar and ordered a martini, he got a call from his secretary.

"Got your text," she said. "Be careful. What are you doing? One of your secret agent missions? I thought you were through with that."

"You never leave the past behind. Anything going on?"

"Madison Hall. She's called five times. Says she had a meeting—I read 'date' into it—with your friend Sheridan and has not been able to find him. Can I please give her your phone number and you can talk to her?"

"Okay. Thanks."

Five minutes later he was speaking to Madison Hall. They decided she'd join him in the hunt for Chummy. She was headed for Acapulco where Chummy might be and couldn't understand why he wasn't answering. She'd stop first in Mexico City and meet Gordon and they could drive together to Acapulco. Later, he'd tell her about the twenty million if she didn't already know. If there was trouble, she'd be good to have along. Had a great right hook and shot a gun better than he did.

Thursday, September 25

On his way to the bank the next morning, Jason Moore checked in. "That photo you sent was definitely Tom Sherwood. He's traveling with the Vice President who, I understand, is in Mexico having meetings some place down on the southern coast. That's all I could learn. But if Sherwood is anxious about the twenty mil, then it might have something to do with that meeting. Maybe your friendly bank manager might have connections or know something."

"Thank you. I'll try and let you know. By the way, Madison Hall's joining me to look for Chummy."

"I don't trust her. I don't like her."

"I feel the same way, but I think her hunt for Chummy is about more than a cancelled date."

✗   ✗   ✗   ✗

The branch manager at Banco de Mexico was waiting for him. Nigel Green had already paved the way and explained the theft of the twenty million.

"I've talked to Nigel. The best I can do right now is freeze the account it's gone into: Arellano Antiques and Art Gallery."

"Appreciate that, but don't freeze it," Gordon said. "Someone went to a great deal of trouble to steal the money. The person the money belongs to may have participated in the theft. Nigel and I need to know where it's going and what it's for. If it leaves the art gallery, let me know where it goes."

"I will do that."

Gordon gave him his contact information.

"I need your help on something else," Gordon said. "I had a call from an investigator who's helping me. He's located a person of interest in this case and this person is at a meeting on the very southern coast of Mexico. The vice president of the United States could be attending. Are you aware of any such meeting? This is all very confidential."

Harris, the branch manager, looked around the room as though he expected someone else to be listening. "There is such a meeting. I have a good friend who is manager of the Inn at Puerto Angel where the meeting is taking place. Very high level. Your vice president, our president, and the president of Guatemala and Nicaragua. They've been getting together off and on over several weeks. The topics the manager hears about are border disputes, illegal aliens, immigrants, terrorism. Very hot."

An area, Gordon thought, that U.S. President Scott Langley didn't have any interest in. "What would it take to get a room at that hotel?"

"I can do that. Tomorrow? I will text you the information."

✗   ✗   ✗   ✗

It was going on noon when Gordon headed back to the hotel. He had spoken to Jason Moore about the meeting in Puerto Angel.

"We'll go tomorrow. But finding Chummy comes first. Let me know if you hear anything else."

"I have. Just a few minutes ago. Osborne's in the hospital. He walked into a moving car."

"I don't think we have to ask how dangerous this is," Gordon said.

"If they tried to kill Osborne, they'll be after Chummy. He has to be warned. Wherever you go, go armed."

He sent a text to Chummy, then returned to the hotel. Madison Hall was waiting for him in the bar, her blond hair pinned back at her neck. Under a baseball cap she looked like any other tourist. They had a quick lunch where they discussed the trip, Chummy and the twenty million, which she already knew about. Before leaving for Acapulco she wanted to stop at a warehouse near the art and antiques district.

"We don't know what we're getting into," she said. "Osborne kept some questionable company. Heard he had an accident last night."

"I just heard the same thing."

They left the hotel and once in the rented Audi, headed for the warehouse district a few blocks away. For Madison, needing to be prepared included two Remington tactical rifles with scopes, three handguns one of which she handed to Gordon, ammunition and some odds and ends. By two-thirty they were on their way south to Acapulco.

All women could learn from Madison, he thought. On time. Well dressed. Even if she was going on a night assault mission. Could handle attackers with the best of them. He never understood the attraction between her and Chummy but it was there … at least off and on.

✗   ✗   ✗   ✗

At a little past seven they pulled into the Holiday Inn Seaside just south of Acapulco. They registered, then headed for the address Nigel Green had given them for Chummy's Acapulco retreat.

Twilight was fading as they drove ten miles south to the village of Barra Vieja. Following directions, Gordon took the first right turn and followed the road as it stretched out to parallel the ocean. Large estates ran along the ocean side. Homes, usually two stories, were on the opposite side of the street. Large chunks of land separated them. Finally they reached the house. A large one story on a corner lot. Opposite was an unpaved road that led to the beach. Gordon pulled into it and parked. They got out and walked across to the house.

"Even at night it looks nice. But I don't see this as Chummy's retreat. More as a place of business," Madison said.

"I agree. It's too off the beaten track. And I don't think he's here."

"We've come this far, let's take a look," Madison said.

A half-dozen palms lined the walk leading to the front door. Madison had her gun in hand. Gordon knocked, then turned the knob. The door moved inward silently. He called Chummy's name. No one answered. He felt along the wall for the light switch. An overhead ceiling light came on. They walked in and found themselves in a foyer decorated with Mexican tile and island-designed furniture. One hall went to the left, the other to the back of the house. Gordon pulled out his gun.

"No one's here," Madison said. "I can feel it."

They searched the house, which was deserted, then went to the back yard. It was large with a lot of trees, regular palms, and a cement patio with a pool. The light came from a post light near the pool and in the rear where a bar was located.

"I see something." Madison headed toward the bar. Gordon followed. On the ground, sprawled near the bar stools was a man dressed in a dark shirt and pants. A straw hat still covered his head.

Gordon lifted the hat. The face was familiar. He'd seen the man on at least one flight and at the hotel. The man had been shot in the head. He reached down to feel the man's chest and found that he wore a bulletproof vest. Who the hell was he? As Gordon turned the body, he touched the skin, which was still warm. The man hadn't died that long ago. He searched his pockets and came up with a black leather folder that told him Harmon Rathburn was a member of the FBI out of the L.A. office. The other thing he found was note paper with the house number.

"What's going on?" He handed the wallet to Madison. "This guy's been following me since I left L.A. On the flight. At the hotel. Why?"

At that moment, a shot buzzed right by his ear. Then came a second directly between them.

"Shit." Gordon took off for the side of the house where the shot came from. Madison ran through the house toward the front street.

"I guess we're getting close to something," Madison said as they met up at the sidewalk. "First the FBI agent, then us. I don't get it."

They took one more walk around the property, searching despite the darkness. It was empty. No footsteps, no voices. The street was silent except for the crash of waves and the hum of traffic from the main highway two blocks away.

"The shooter stood outside and used the fence for support," Gordon said. "He had to know he wouldn't be seen or didn't care if he was."

"I guess he's gone. I hope. Probably parked in town. I don't suppose we're reporting this?" she asked.

"To whom?"

As they walked back to the car, Madison looked around. "I still can't believe this is Chummy's Acapulco retreat. It's nice. But it's not him. Who gave you this address?"

"Nigel Green."

"And I guess he got it from Chummy. Chummy lies a lot you know," she said. "Any guess why the FBI agent was here? And why the killer was shooting at us?"

"Maybe this is all about drugs. Twenty million fits in perfectly. What if Chummy's an importer and something went wrong?"

Friday, September 26

The hour-and-fifteen-minute flight from Acapulco to Tapachula left at ten a.m. Madison slept and Gordon continued to search for answers to the riddle of the twenty million. The names of those attending the meetings at the Puerto Angel Inn included vice president Michael Springer, his chief of staff and two secret service agents; Carlos Reynosa, president of Mexico and two bodyguards; Ricardo Bartholomew, president of Guatemala, and his two aides; and Leon Somoto, president of Nicaragua and two aides.

Gordon could understand that the reason for the meetings was the growing common problem of immigrants and terrorism. But how did the twenty million fit in?

"What is Tapachula known for, do you know?" Madison asked.

"From what I read, coffee plantations, agriculture, medicine, technology. The population is German and Chinese as well as Mexican."

"It doesn't sound like anything to do with Chummy's money."

"Not unless he was buying a coffee plantation. Or was involved in drugs. There's a large port just up the coast."

✗   ✗   ✗   ✗

The Tapachula airport was about fifteen miles from Puerto Angel. They rented another Audi and started along route 225, which led south toward Puerto Angel. The village was comprised of a boulevard that bordered the ocean and several smaller streets that crisscrossed it. Shops, restaurants, car repair and other businesses, including two hotels and a church, dotted the landscape. At the intersection, Gordon turned left and two miles later where the road ended, the Inn at Puerto Angel appeared.

The hotel, a large white stucco three-story building with a dark blue tile roof, was set back among tall palms and flowering shrubs. He pulled into the circle and stopped in front of the entrance guarded by two polished mahogany doors. It was just before noon.

"Very nice," Madison said. "It's great we could get a room here."

"Right in the heart of whatever's going on."

Gordon handed the car keys to the valet. The hotel interior was pleasantly tropical and a small bar where wine and beer were served was tucked into a corner. The manager Francesco Cortez was waiting for them. A man of medium height with gray peppering his dark hair, his smile showed straight white teeth. He was impeccably dressed in a dark blue suit. He was friendly, but there was an air of caution in his manner. Gordon wondered how much of their situation and the twenty million the bank manager had told him.

After greeting them, Cortez mentioned a reception at seven for all guests. "Miguel will show you to your room. If you have any questions, please let me know."

Their second-floor room, decorated with tile floors, dark wood furniture and white fabrics, had a view of the pool and harbor. It was comfortable, with two double beds and a small sitting room with sofa.

"Do you have a plan?" Madison opened a bottle of water and walked out onto the terrace.

"No. How can we find something when we don't know what it is?"

"Do you mind if I leave the sleuthing to you this afternoon? I saw a sign in the lobby for a spa and hair salon in Tapachula. The hotel provides transportation. They're leaving at one."

"Go ahead. I'm going to grab lunch and walk around. Who knows what I'll find."

After Madison left, Gordon went down to the main floor where the bar and lounge were located. A few guests sat at the bar or tables scattered about the room. Mexican art and tapestries hung from the white walls and a long mahogany bar was lighted by two elaborate chandeliers. He sat at the end where he could see the entrance. He was halfway through his beer when a man in his late thirties/early forties walked in. He had dark hair and looked fit and trim in his brown pants and white polo shirt. Gordon had seen him yesterday sitting across the table from Francis Osborne. Tom Sherwood.

Sherwood looked around the partially-filled room, then walked over and took a seat next to Gordon. "Remember me? Tom Sherwood. We met at that security seminar about a year ago."

Suddenly Gordon realized why Sherwood looked familiar. "Yes. You were with the Secret Service. Are you still with them?"

"I still work for the vice president, but in a different capacity. He's here along with the presidents of Mexico, Guatemala, and Nicaragua. They're meeting regarding the issues of refugees, border problems, and terrorism."

"And President Langley says there's no problem. It's all in everyone's imagination." Gordon sipped his beer and watched Sherwood's expression.

"Which is why we're here without him. They're working to develop a uniform policy which they hope other countries will follow. Langley's viewpoint paralyzes any forward movement which the U.S. and other countries need. These are not issues on which our country and others can afford to wait until Langley gets on board. Unfortunately, Langley found out about the meetings and has forced his way in. He'll be arriving tonight around seven."

"Langley's coming uninvited?"

Sherwood nodded.

"That can't be good."

"It isn't."

So the president's going to be here, Gordon thought. As he watched Sherwood walk away, he wondered if he had anything to do with Osborne's accident. Probably. The president barging in was a setting for disaster.

With that thought lingering he placed another call to Chummy and when his friend didn't answer, he sent a text. The feeling that something was wrong gnawed at him. How could Chummy just vanish?

Following a hunch, he called the one person who would know where Chummy's money went: his tax accountant.

"I went to the house in Barra Vieja," Gordon told him. "It's a really nice place, but I can't believe that's where Chummy goes for a long weekend. He's really not the type who wants to get away from it all."

"I was there once. Nice. He rents it out a couple of months a year to pay expenses. But that's not his retreat. It's a smaller house in the hills above Acapulco Bay." He gave Gordon the address.

Gordon jotted it down. Chummy had been missing since late Tuesday. His airline ticket said Acapulco. Did he make it there? He needed someone to go to the house and take a look. He headed for the manager's office. He knocked and at the 'come in,' did just that.

They chatted for a few minutes about nothing in particular, then Gordon asked how he'd go about getting police help in Acapulco.

"I was a member of the Mexican police for many years," Cortez answered. "That's what I did before becoming manager here. I started out as security. When they needed someone to run the place, I jumped in. Why do you need the police?"

"A friend is missing. He may have gone to his house in Acapulco a few days back. I was hoping the police could send someone to check if he's there. It's odd for him to be out of touch this long."

"Let me make a call. I need a name and an address, if you have it."

Gordon gave him both. "Please let me know what you find."

Unable to stand the wait, Gordon went outside by the pool and called Detective Maia Alcott from the twentieth precinct in Manhattan. "Did you get my alibi for the time of Robin Glasser's death?" he said when she answered.

"I did. You were confirmed as being at a client meeting. There was no need to bother you directly."

"What do you have on her murder? The gun in particular."

"Ballistics have it as a Sig Sauer P239. Bullets match. Do you know where Charles Sheridan is? He's a possible suspect."

"He could be in Acapulco. I've asked for help from the Acapulco police. Chummy hasn't answered a phone call, an email, or a text since Tuesday."

"Where in Mexico are you?"

"At a meeting on the coast." He was about to say something else when someone knocked on his door. "I need to answer the door. I'll call you back in a few minutes."

It was a summons to the manager's office.

"Mr. Sheridan was in his home," the manager began. "He's been dead since shortly after his arrival on Wednesday. He was shot with a Sig Sauer P239."

"Did anyone see anything?" Gordon asked.

"No. Have you any information?"

"Detective Alcott from Manhattan's twentieth precinct is investigating a murder where the same type weapon was used. The woman killed was a friend of Charles Sheridan's."

Cortez was on the phone immediately to the Acapulco police. "They're getting in touch with her now." He stayed on the line, nodding his head. "Interesting," he said. "I'll ask him. He's here in my office. The police pulled another address for Mr. Sheridan. They investigated and found another body. This time, an FBI agent. Looks like he was shot some time yesterday. Any idea who this man might be?"

"No," Gordon answered. He sent a text to Jason regarding Chummy.

Someone came to the door. "Excuse me for a moment," the manager said. "Sometimes I forget we have a hotel to run."

While the manager walked into the next room, Gordon looked around. Plaques, framed articles, and photos hung on the wall. As he waited, he glanced at the articles, stopping at one with a 1982 date. The article was about a 'friendly fire' incident involving the CIA that took place in Mexico near Guatemala. A name, Manuel Cortez, was highlighted in yellow. Must be Francesco's father, he thought.

The event involved gold that had been stolen from Japan during World War II and had made its way into Guatemala and Mexico, among other places. A group of mercenaries, later identified as CIA, were there to transport it back to the States. Dissention in the group led to a gun fight. One group, led by Scott Langley, fired on the other group. One of the men killed was identified as George Madison Hall.

Gordon stared at the article. Scott Langley killed George Madison Hall. Madison's father? It took a minute for the fact to set in. He remembered the event from early in his military career. He called Jason Moore.

"Do you know anything about Madison Hall's father? I'm looking at an article from Mexico City's *El Diario*, dated 1982. It was hanging on the wall in the hotel manager's office. It looks like his father was a part of the army who battled the mercenaries, as they were called."

"I know Madison's father did undercover work for the government. I don't think anyone admitted to being CIA. And yes, he could have been killed in Mexico. Why?"

"I can't believe this. The article says that among the men Scott Langley killed in the 'friendly fire' exchange was George Madison Hall. That's her father. That's what this is all about."

"Our current president killed her father in that gun battle? That's unbelievable. You think Madison plans to get even?"

"Yes. She plans to assassinate the President of the United States," Gordon said.

"Except that's not how she sees it," Jason pointed out. "She's avenging her father's murder. Is Langley coming there?"

"Tonight at seven. That's what Chummy's twenty million is all about. Madison needed it to get the right people to put Langley in a position where she could get at him. Takes a lot of money to do that. And that's why we picked up those tactical rifles in Mexico City. She's probably been planning this for a long time."

"But how did Chummy get involved?"

"She went to him for the money. He might even have said 'yes.' Then got cold feet and thought it was over. I can only imagine his surprise when I told him the twenty million was gone from his account. He knew exactly what happened to it. He called Madison, then rerouted the money. After that he went to the FBI. That explains why the agent was trailing us. He was after Madison."

"Is there anything you can do?"

"Stop her. I don't know how. But I've got to try something. She left for Tapachula when we got here. That was a lie. She's probably out scouting locations and getting set up. I'm sure her accomplice is Tom Sherwood."

"You're walking into a history-making situation. Just come out of this alive. And don't get picked up by the Secret Service."

"I'll try not to."

Cortez walked into the office. "I overheard most of your conversation. I'm shocked. You really think that woman who came with you is here to kill your president?"

"He killed her father." Gordon handed him the article.

"And you want to stop her? How?"

"I have no idea. But I've got to get to the airport."

"I'm coming with you," Cortez stated. "The staff can take care of the reception. I can get us into the airport and near the president, where you can't."

✗ ✗ ✗ ✗

On the half-hour ride to the Tapachula Airport, Gordon received a text from Marco Harris. It said: *Twenty million gone. Moved from art gallery account to American Bank with a branch in Tapachula. That's all I can tell you.*

Madison had paid her debts.

✗ ✗ ✗ ✗

It was still light as they approached the modern two-story structure. Behind it, at the southern edge of the Sierra Madre, an extinct volcano rose. They went inside the terminal. There was no activity except for a few airport personnel. It was six forty-five. A security guard gave them a ride to the landing area.

"The flight's on time," Cortez told him. He was wearing very impressive police credentials and had given similar ones to Gordon to wear on his navy blazer. "The only incoming flight is the one carrying your president."

At seven o'clock, the unmarked Gulfstream landed on the main runway. It taxied to the north approach, which brought the plane to the far end of the airport, away from the terminal and surrounded by trees and long stretches of grasslands. The only place for a sniper was the top of the terminal, but security had that under control. Gordon had the feeling Madison chose a location with a better escape route. By the time five members of the secret service and the President deplaned, night was rapidly descending.

President Langley came down the steps, then stopped as Cortez walked up and greeted him. Gordon couldn't believe that no one stopped him. They shook hands, then Langley headed to the limousine, surrounded by secret service.

Gordon watched, wondering how many agents were friends of Madison's. He glanced at the time. It had been five minutes since the President walked down the stairs. So far, there was not enough opportunity to get off a shot. The group proceeded toward the waiting limo. Within a minute Langley would be inside the car.

Then without warning, the limousine pulled away, stopping a few yards closer to the terminal. Without the shield of the car, Langley was exposed. This was the plan. *Now* is when they'll shoot. Realizing what was going to happen, Gordon did something he never thought he would do: he sprinted across the open space heading for the President, willing to put himself in front of the sniper's bullet. The first shot caught Gordon in the arm as he tried to cover Langley. The second shot caught Langley between the eyes.

Gordon fell on the ground next to the President. For a moment everyone stood in shock. The agents looked around. There were no crowds to dispel, no press to hold back, no orders to give. No gunman visible. Except for the two shots, the area was quiet and deserted.

Gordon got to his feet with the help of Cortez and immediately wrapped the arms of his jacket around the wound. Cortez called the chief of police in Tapachula, the hospital, then the hotel.

"There's a regional hospital a mile from here," he said to the agents. "They're sending an ambulance. The medical examiner will meet you there. I've also called the hotel to inform your vice president." Then he turned to Gordon. "That wound needs immediate care. There's nothing we can do for Langley."

The lead agent came up and thanked Gordon and said his deed would be remembered.

"I hope not," Gordon whispered to Cortez as they walked away.

✗   ✗   ✗   ✗

"We'll keep you overnight," the nurse said to Gordon as he sat in one of the hospital's emergency examination rooms, "just to make sure no infection is setting in. Are you his next of kin?" she asked Cortez, handing him the form to sign.

"For now." He laughed.

"You know, I've been thinking about the last few days," Gordon said once the nurse left. "I think there's a bigger picture here. Madison did a lot of bad things for what she thought was a good reason. Robin Glasser's dead. My friend Chummy … I feel really, really bad about that. And about Francis Osborne, who's still in the hospital. You know, the country is in trouble. Ours, yours, all of Central America. Any country where terrorists can enter with ease. The people meeting in Puerto Angel were working for the common good, and Michael Springer was not about to let Scott Langley undo all the progress they've made. It was time for a change. The good of the many outweighed the good of the few."

"So you're saying Michael Springer was behind this?" Cortez furrowed his brow, then nodded his head slowly. "I can see it. He might have known Madison's father. He decided it was time to put an end to Langley. He called on her and she jumped at the chance for revenge. There were a few casualties along the way, but I suppose that's the price that needs to be paid. The course of history was changed here today. But no one will remember Puerto Angel."

"I don't agree. The press will not let them forget it. Just think of how busy your hotel is going to be."

Saturday, October 25

The trees were nearly bare and the ground had already seen its first frost in East Hampton. Chummy was buried in a small cemetery outside the town. He loved that area more than anywhere else. Gordon stood at the graveside. Next to him was Nigel Green.

Gordon brought a plant for which he dug a hole. Hardly anything grew in East Hampton during the winter, but the small evergreen might stand a chance. Nigel placed a wreath against the headstone.

"He fought for his country," Nigel said. "And he ended up dying for it. But not in a way anyone would ever know or remember. Except a few."

"It's lonely out here. Maybe in the summer someone will remember him and drop by. But I doubt it. I wonder about Madison. The only people to connect Michael Springer to Langley's murder are Tom Sherwood and Madison. Sherwood's a dirty trickster, so he's useful. Madison's a loose end. I hope she knows that. But if she's been planning this for a while, then she's also set a course for a secure future."

"Where do you think she went?" Nigel asked.

"She's in Guatemala. Cut her hair. Dyed it black, and is on the hunt for the missing gold that her father and Langley left behind."

"I hope she finds it."

"So do I."

✗

Dianne Neral Ell has written professionally for trade and consumer publications, online magazines and websites. Her short stories have appeared in anthologies and *Sherlock Holmes Mystery Magazine*. *The Exhibit*, a novel of crime and suspense, is currently available at most retailers including Amazon and Barnes and Noble. She is a member of the Mystery Writers of America, the Author's Guild and the Florida Writers Association. Her website is: www.dianneneralell.com.

TAKE-OUT

by Laird Long

The punk spun around on the sun-baked sidewalk and blasted two shots from his .38 special lead-dispenser at the car tailing him. The windshield of the Monte Carlo SS exploded, bathing the large man at the wheel in a wave of glass. The big guy slammed on the brakes and piled out of the car. The punk turned the corner at top speed and ran down an alley. The temperature in Vegas was one hundred and fifteen degrees.

"Dammit," grumbled the big guy in the white open-necked shirt, blue dress pants and black brogues. When you're six foot six and three hundred and twenty pounds, a foot chase ain't your gig, especially in the baker's oven that was mid-summer Las Vegas.

The big man rumbled around the corner after the punk, sweat streaming down his cheeks. A hot wind stuck grit to his wet face. The punk was caged at the end of the shaded lane, trapped by a twenty-foot-high fence. The punk turned around to face his tormentor, now a giant silhouette bearing down on him. The punk was juiced on crack and booze. He tried to level the rod in his shaking mitts.

The big man drew a Glock 9 mm from his shoulder harness and blasted a hole in the punk's leg. The punk hit the cement yelping like a dog just run over. The big man applied the brakes and walked up to the punk squealing on the ground. He kicked the punk's gun away from where it slumbered. He then kicked the punk in the ribs with one of his size fourteens. The sound of three ribs fracturing sounded good to the big man, sounded like retribution for the busted windshield.

"Hey, man! Whatcha' doin'?" the punk screamed in agony, his red, bleary eyes bugging out of his haggard, drug-addled face.

"I don't like running," the big man calmly replied. With his left hand he picked the bloody punk up by the front of his Raiders T-shirt. "And I just had my car fixed last week," he added. With his right fist, he smashed the punk's face, busting a couple of teeth and putting an end to the whining the best way he knew how.

✗   ✗   ✗   ✗

The big guy finished up the paperwork at the cop shop.

"Hey, Deck, you tracing skips now?" the cop in the too-tight uniform asked him.

"The P.I. business isn't as hot as your weather, right now," Deck Winters replied glumly.

"Maybe you should think about becoming a policeman," the cop cracked.

"Naw, I can't afford the cut in pay. Besides, I got a thing about clip-on ties and polyester suits."

The cop laughed. "You know, I still remember that game against St. Louis when you tangled with Dave 'The Animal' Ewing …"

Deck waved good-bye before the cop could finish his skate down memory lane. Deck wasn't in the mood for old hockey war stories. He just wanted to get home. Where the heat didn't pin your clothes to your body in a wet sticky embrace.

✗   ✗   ✗   ✗

Deck drove his windshield-less car over to a convenience store to pick up some gum. The hot air stung his face like a whip. How the hell can anyone live in this heat, he wondered, as he walked into the chill of the air-conditioned store.

He picked up his sugar-free chew sticks and ambled over to the counter. Since he had forsaken booze and the rolled leaves, his maw was never without a big wad of gum. Blowing bubbles kept him occupied when he was bouncing at the Waddling Duck in the Twin Cities or when he was out on an actual stake-out on an actual job.

He spilled the requisite silverware on the counter. The pimply runt of a clerk wasn't interested.

"Hey, Mister, could you maybe talk to that guy over there?" He pointed a wavering digit at the back of the store. "He's been roughing up his girlfriend ever since they came in. I don't want no trouble."

Deck sighed. His size came in handy in his vocation, but it also meant that every citizen with a bully viewed him as his or her own personal savior, or as an off-duty cop.

He rubbed a big paw over his crew-cut and turned around for a look. Sure enough, a tall skinny black guy, probably a pimp, was pushing around a petite blonde of dubious repute. They were arguing about something. Deck steamed their way.

"Bitch, you been stiffin' me," the black guy in the hundred-dollar white suit said. His gold teeth glinted in the lenses of the security cameras. He pushed the blonde into a display of potato chips, knocking the bags and the blonde to the floor.

"Buddy, why don't you take it easy on the junk food?" Deck inquired, a grin on his face.

Skinny did a three-sixty, something nasty to say on his lips. His jaws clamped shut like the legs of a virgin when he gazed at the immensity of Deck.

"S-sure man, I'm cool," he stuttered.

The blonde picked herself up off the floor and seized the moment to sucker-punch her business associate in the jaw. He hit the floor, out cold.

"Thanks, anyway," she said to Deck. "But I can handle myself." She tugged at her short-shorts and adjusted the stretched-to-the-limit tank top she was barely wearing. "Maybe I can handle you, too?" she asked, a smile on her pouty red lips.

"I only came for the gum," Deck replied. He exited the store shaking his head in amazement.

He drove his open-air vehicle just past the city limits, then pulled into Hookers for a bite to eat. He also needed a few gallons of water to replace the stuff leaking out every pore on his body. As he walked to the heavy wooden door of the coffee shop/gambling casino/strip joint/gas station/car wash, he cased the parking lot. Deck made it a habit never to let his eyes stop moving.

Hookers was owned by Johnny Hooker, local low-life made good. Vegas was the city of second chances, after all. Deck heard that there was always a lot of cash at Hookers, but Johnny had an aversion to robbery, so he kept an arsenal of weapons behind every counter. There had been a couple of shoot-outs since the joint opened up, and all ended with Johnny holding onto his dough.

Deck made a wrong turn at the entrance to the amusement park and found himself in the cool, smoke-darkened confines of the strip club. A silicon-enhanced brunette was caressing her tanned body on the big stage, while her naked colleagues danced on stools in front of tables of men and some women scattered throughout the club.

Deck reversed and hit the right door. He walked into the spacious, bright, fifties-style coffee shop and plunked his tired body down into a vinyl-covered booth. He eye-balled Johnny before the entrepreneur disappeared into an office off to the side of the long counter.

Deck cracked open the plastic-covered menu and surveyed his options.

"What can I get you?" a pretty redhead in a tight pink uniform asked him before long. "You are one big fella," she added. "If you don't mind me saying so."

"I'm big all over," he grinned.

She blushed and took his order.

Deck was thinking about where he could get his car repaired when a man with a black balaclava pulled over his head stormed in. Odd attire for this time of year.

"Okay, everyone grab some tile!" the guy yelled. He held a laundry bag in his left hand while his right clutched an ugly black .357 Magnum.

Nobody moved.

"Hit the floor, morons!" the man yelled.

This time the customers and the serving staff got the message, and they dove to the floor, covering their heads. A woman screamed in the back.

Deck calmly gazed at the dude in the ski mask, pulled off his thick glasses and rubbed his eyes. What a day.

"That means you too, big boy!" Jean-Claude Killy screamed in Deck's direction.

Just then Johnny burst out of his office, anger painted on his face.

"What the hell do you think you're doing?" he yelled at the man with the gun.

"I want the cash you have in your office, Johnny," the man replied.

"I got a policy, punk," Johnny said as he took in the situation. "No refunds."

Johnny edged towards the counter to try to reach one of the weapons he kept as a deterrent to inventory shrinkage.

"You give me the cash or I start blowing away your customers, pal."

Johnny shoved his hairy arms in the air. "Hey, take it easy, brother. Like I said, you ain't gettin' any of my money. I let you have it, then everyone wants it. You see how that would be bad for business?"

Deck didn't cotton to the way this game was unfolding. It was the irresistible force meeting the immovable object, with innocent patrons maybe getting crushed in the collision.

"I figured you be a hard-ass, Johnny." The guy with the big gun calmly walked over to a young woman cowering on the floor. She was rolled up into the fetal position, whimpering with fright.

"Johnny just signed your death certificate, sister," the tough in the toque said purposefully.

The woman must have known he was serious because she let out a scream and made a break for the door. The .357 exploded in protest. The woman hit the floor three yards from Deck, blood rapidly staining her pretty white summer dress.

The other customers screamed. The stick-up man meant business, even Johnny could see that now.

"Okay, okay," he said, his voice cracking just a bit. He realized that dead customers didn't pay their lunch bills and word-of-mouth was murder. "I'll get the money."

"Hold it, Johnny," Deck ordered.

All eyes turned towards the big man in the corner booth, waiting patiently for his double cheeseburger. Deck squeezed out of the booth and stood up.

"You wanna die, hero?" the killer yelled at him. The big gun looked directly at Deck with its one good eye.

"I want to eat," Deck replied. "Besides, no one's going to die, sonny-boy. Unless Johnny's not grilling the burgers long enough."

Johnny jumped in. "Friend, I appreciate your help and all, but I think you'd better park it. This bum is the real deal."

"This bum has a diaper rash that five years in the pen might cure," Deck said. He strode over to the bloody hostage stretched out on the cold floor. He crushed the heel of his shoe down onto her limp right hand. Bones snapped. The corpse moaned in agony.

"Get away from her!" the guy with a stocking for a hat yelled protectively. He advanced on Deck with the peacemaker.

Deck roughly scooped up the woman's purse, almost tearing her arm off, searched through it and pulled out a gun. "I think this works a bit better than yours, pal," he said. He pointed a tiny silver .22 at the robber.

They faced each other, fifty feet between them, guns pointed at each other's heads. Deck's gun looked puny compared to the monster the crook was holding. Judgment day had come to Hookers. The woman on the floor rolled over and screamed an obscenity at Deck. She cradled her wrecked gun hand like a baby.

"What the hell's going on?" Johnny asked, as confused as anyone.

"I saw these two parked outside before I came in, Johnny," Deck answered. "Our friend here with the woolen head-condom wanted to convince you he was serious, so he got his girlfriend to perform an acting job straight out of Bonnie & Clyde. Complete with exploding cherry juice. It's the only way he could convince you to go unleaded on a robbery for a change. I'm betting that the big shot with the big gun has nothing but blanks."

"You're in the wrong town if you bet like that, Mister," the crook replied. He squeezed the trigger on his big iron and the window behind Deck fragmented into a million pieces. It could have been Deck's head.

Deck was about to counter with the pop-gun when Johnny pulled a sawed-off from behind the counter and blasted away. The crook was thrown to the ground like a ragdoll by the force of the explosions. His dead body skidded to a halt in front of the doors marked 'Exit.'

"Thanks for your help, Tiny," Johnny said to Deck. "I guess he only had the one blank in the gun."

"Yeah," Deck replied shakily. He suddenly remembered the cool peace of his home in the Land of 10,000 Lakes, far removed from the Wild West show they were running out here. "Can I get my order 'to go'?" he asked.

✗

Laird Long: Big guy, sense of humor; pounds out fiction in all genres. Has appeared in many anthologies and mystery magazines and resides in Winnipeg, Canada.

NERO WOLFE, PRO BONO

by Archie Goodwin

transcribed by Marvin Kaye

When Sergeant Purley Stebbins of the NYPD pays us a visit, it is usually unannounced and confrontational. But one morning shortly after lunch, the phone rang and it was him. He asked to speak with Wolfe, who was in his chair drinking beer. I told him who was on the line and since we had no clients and weren't on a case, he was as surprised as I was.

"Yes, Sergeant?" he asked.

"I need to see you as soon as possible."

"For what purpose?"

"I'd rather tell you in person."

"Very well. I can fit you in at 2:30."

Purley thanked him and hung up.

"Fit him in?" I asked. "You've got nothing to do but play with orchids at four o'clock."

"No one needs to know we're currently—how shall I put it?"

"Unemployed. What do you think he wants?"

Wolfe shrugged, for him a workout. "Pointless to speculate." He turned his attention to beer and the mail, in that order.

⚡   ⚡   ⚡   ⚡

After lunch I went to Murray Street near City Hall to buy shoe polish for Wolfe. I barely got back in time to open the door for Purley and got a shock. Not only was he not in uniform, he was in a black suit and bowtie that was all wrong for him.

For once he sat in the red leather chair, which made me curious enough to ask.

"That's where you always seat your clients."

"Otherwise your boss sits there." I rang for Wolfe, who entered and offered him beer. He usually said no, but this time he said thank you and waited for Fritz to bring him a pilsner glass and a bottle of Remmers. Purley filled the glass, raised it and said, "To Inspector Cramer."

We repeated him, then Wolfe asked why we were toasting him. "Has something bad happened?"

"Yes, but he's not sick and he hasn't been hurt. I want to hire you, Wolfe."

"To do what?"

"Defend the inspector. He's been arrested."

"*What?!*" That was me. "What for?"

"Murder. I know it's going to cost me a year's salary."

"Not necessarily," Wolfe replied. "Archie, your notebook."

⚔ ⚔ ⚔ ⚔

Purley laid it out for us. They'd arrested a rape-murderer named Jack Gainslee and he was being interrogated by Cramer and an assistant DA named Perry Benjamin. At one point, Benjamin left the room to use the john. When he got back, Cramer was on the floor unconscious and Gainslee had a bullet in what was left of his skull. According to Cramer, he'd been waiting for Benjamin to return to continue the interrogation, but suddenly the door opened and someone slugged him and he passed out. The next thing he knew the assistant DA was shaking him. They recovered the bullet. It fitted the inspector's weapon, which held only his fingerprints.

"Sergeant," Wolfe asked, "isn't it possible that—?"

"No! Never!"

"I agree with you, but if I find evidence supporting his guilt, you know I will not be able to ignore or suppress it."

Purley got out his checkbook. "How much?"

"One dollar."

"As a retainer?"

"No, that's the entire fee."

Purley rose to shake his hand, remembered that Wolfe didn't like doing that and also must have remembered that he likes eyes on his own level since he sat back down and thanked him.

With the almost invisible lip twist that passed for a smile, Wolfe said, "If I succeed, I will expect Mr. Cramer—no, not money—I'll want him to do me a favor. Details only if and when he is exonerated."

While we waited for the trial date to be set, Wolfe kept me busy checking on the victim and how many people might want him dead. Fred Durkin, with Purley's help, investigated Cramer, while our best operative Saul Panzer worked on the assistant DA. We all figured we'd be called as witnesses.

Now if you read the case I wrote up as "The Next Witness," you know that Wolfe hates to be called to court for several reasons: the long waiting involved, being made to sit on a bench next to a stranger and if it's a woman, being forced to endure what he calls repellent perfume (it doesn't matter if she's not wearing any).

The day that the trial began, I was in the second row, which took some doing to make happen; it broke the rule that witnesses had to wait some place else, but Wolfe said he would not do anything unless I was there, so Cramer's attorney Aaron Golzer (recommended by Wolfe's legal representative Nat Parker) met with the prosecutor and the judge and explained that Wolfe was vital to his case and at last the judge allowed it, subject to her reevaluation if anything happened and she deemed it necessary to clear the courtroom.

So there I was in the second row. Wolfe was up front sitting next to Cramer and Golzer, who'd found a chair big enough to accommodate Wolfe's fundament, not that it (the chair) didn't groan about it.

"All rise!" an officer proclaimed and we all rose for the judge, a Number Ten on the heart-flutter scale named Carolyn Grove. She took her place on the bench and the trial began. The opening business is pretty much the same in all American courtrooms, so I'll skip ahead to the calling of witnesses. The prosecutor had three: the officer stationed in the hall, the assistant DA Perry Benjamin, and Inspector Cramer, who overrode counsel's advice and agreed to take the stand, which he did after the officer cum hall monitor answered a few questions that bore out what I'd already learned— other than the assistant D.A., Inspector Cramer, and of course the prisoner, no one else entered or left the vicinity.

The officer stepped down and Cramer was sworn in. The prosecutor, whose name was Rufus Claridge, ascertained the inspector's name and rank, then asked how long he'd been with the NYPD.

"Now please describe the events leading up to Mr. Benjamin's discovery of the body."

Cramer did so in great detail. Of course Claridge hammered away at every bit of testimony, but he couldn't shake his story. All in all, Cramer's testimony provided nothing negative to the State, though nothing positive, either.

The prosecutor called his final witness. Perry Benjamin took the stand and was sworn in. I noticed Wolfe murmuring something to Golzer the defense attorney, who nodded yes.

✗ ✗ ✗ ✗

Maybe I should have told you some things that happened before the trial, so now we've got to back-track so I can tell you what Wolfe did once he accepted Purley Stebbins's case. The first thing he did was assign me and Saul Panzer and Fred Durkin to find out as soon as we could what other people had motives to kill the rapist/victim Jack Gainslee. It took two days (which I think shows how good we are!) and another day to narrow down the field, which was large. At last I told Wolfe we'd narrowed it down to three of the likeliest suspects.

"Satisfactory." But then he frowned. "Archie, do you think that we should also look into whoever might hold animus for Mr. Cramer?"

"I thought about that, Chief, but I think it's a long shot. We can always do it if nothing else works out."

"I agree. Summon the three suspects as soon as possible so I may—"

"I already have. They'll be here tonight at nine."

"Most satisfactory!"

"High praise … is a raise in order?"

He chuckled. "I have already expressed my esteem for your efforts, Archie. Nothing more need be added, for as has been said, virtue is its own reward."

"Not at the supermarket, it isn't."

✗ ✗ ✗ ✗

The trio arrived promptly at nine. There were two men, Carter deVane and Leon Jefferson, and one woman, Belinda Benowicz, who immediately claimed the red leather chair and before I could offer drinks, requested a double over ice of Michter's rye, which I assumed she saw we had. The men chose scotch, not generically, but Ballantine (Jefferson) and a brandy snifter of the hard-to-find (in America) Glen Turret single malt for Carter deVane. I was impressed with their choices and hoped none of them were guilty.

A few physical details to set the scene: Jefferson wore blue jeans and a dark T-shirt, which was quite a contrast to deVane's costly gray suit, off-white shirt, and slim tie affixed by a diamond-chip clip. Oddly, he wore paddock boots, which suggested that he rode horses. (By the way, I should mention that he was—is—*the* Carter deVane, whose name and business ventures were frequently associated with *Fortune 500*.)

Belinda's garb was, I regret to report, mannish. Black shirt and tie (!), tight black slacks that earned for her that characterization popular, I'm told, somewhere in Africa as callipygian.

Wolfe entered and I introduced the three of them. Belinda corrected me when I called her "Miss Benowicz"—I should have foreseen she should be referred to as "Ms."

When I introduced Leon Jefferson, Wolfe actually shook his hand, or at least brushed against it. "I have read your excellent history of the Civil War, sir—you certainly deserved the Pulitzer Prize. Your subject, after all, has formed the core of many books, but you found both new information and insights. I congratulate you."

"Mr. Wolfe," Jefferson said, "your praise has made this visit worthwhile!"

Everyone took their seats and after the inevitable beer ritual, Wolfe opened his mouth to begin the proceedings, but was interrupted by Ms. B.B., who hoped she'd have an opportunity to see his orchids. Now that's a request that always pleases him, but not this time. He ignored her remark and embarked, instead, on a preliminary statement to the trio. Obviously, he didn't care for her, but why? He couldn't already have chosen her as the murderer—no questions had yet been asked of anyone.

Well, the next half-hour was taken up with him finding out their reasons for wanting to kill Jack Gainslee. Belinda admitted that she was a rape victim, but didn't want to provide any details. "It's embarrassing—no, it's *humiliating* to talk about it in a roomful of men."

"I see that," Wolfe said. "Can you tell me this, though? Was your rapist ever caught?"

She smiled, which I thought unsettling. "He's dead."

"How did he die? Did you—?"

"No, Mr. Wolfe. My brother did it."

"Indeed?!" His eyebrows shot up. "Who—?"

"No," she cut in, "that's all I'm going to say about it. It's over and done with and I'm glad. No more questions." She asked me for a rye refill, which I got for her.

Wolfe gave it up. Turning to Leon Jefferson, he said "I have no basis to think this, sir, but you do not strike me as a murderer."

Jefferson stroked his white mustache and sipped his scotch. "Mr. Wolfe, I should think that you of all people would know that everyone on this planet is at least potentially a murderer. My cousin Ruth, who I adored, was raped and they never caught the bastard. If I could have killed him, I would have. Now you may well ask whether that experience would prompt me to kill another such monster, even if I did not know him. The answer is yes, I would, even if I knew I would be caught and punished for it. But Mr. Wolfe, I am really a very lazy fellow—"

"I find that hard to believe. Your Civil War history must have taken ever so much energy to research and write."

Jefferson nodded. "That's true. But I *enjoyed* the process! Still, if I found myself in the same room with a known rapist, I would not hesitate to do him in. But I was nowhere near this Gainslee fellow. I was in London at that time, and before you ask it, yes, I have witnesses."

A sound somewhere between a grunt and a snort was produced by Carter deVane. We turned to him as he said, "I, on the other hand, was actually in the neighborhood of the building where the Gainslee murder happened … and I have no witnesses to say I did not go inside and kill him. Which I would have done. He raped my sister, but she would not testify against him in court."

It ended soon after that. I saw them all out, locked the door and returned to the office, where Wolfe sat with his eyes closed and his lips doing their in-out dance. But it was a short set, choreographically. He looked at me and said, "Archie, what are your impressions of what we heard?"

"Not much. The only thing I wonder about is the details that Belinda wouldn't share."

He nodded. "My thoughts, precisely. Jefferson, of course, we can dismiss since he was in London and you may be certain he'll be able to prove it." He rang for beer and when Fritz entered, Wolfe surprised us both by not specifying which brand to bring. "Surprise me."

Fritz and I exchanged a startled glance and as he went out, I said, "Who are you and what have you done with Mr. Wolfe?"

"I'm merely celebrating the prospect of clearing Mr. Cramer."

"You've solved it?!"

An elephantine sigh. "I have a theory. But I need evidence."

That meant work for me and maybe Saul and/or Fred, but before I could ask Fritz returned with a bottle of Angry Bastard and a second one of Iron City beer, which a client sent Wolfe from Pittsburgh.

He began with Angry Bastard, which did not match his mood. He tasted it and said, "Satisfactory," which promptly sent Fritz to heaven, at that moment situated in our kitchen. To me Wolfe said, "Tomorrow you will ask Saul to investigate deVane who was, after all, near the murder scene. But the fact that he volunteered that information is in his favor."

"OK, but I can do it, you know."

"No, Archie, I need you to dig into the untold details of Ms. Belinda's violation." He shuddered. "I detest that word. *Ms.* It sounds like the echo of a bee's drone." He opened and poured Iron City beer, adjusted the bead and took a sip. "Oh, good grief!" he exclaimed, eyes wide. "I never thought I'd declare a beer undrinkable, but *this*—is an abomination!"

He picked up the bottle, which I thought he was about to smash, but instead he poured the rest into his glass and drank it.

"If it's so bad, why did you—?"

"I thought I'd been too hard on it and gave it a second chance. And now I know what Hell tastes like!"

✗　✗　✗　✗

Back to the trial … the shortest one I ever witnessed. This was partly because the prosecutor's case was brief and Wolfe's (Golzer's) even more so. It occurred to me that my werowance

(American Indian for "Chief," the only word I ever stumped him with) was in court *pro bono*, which is against his religion, if he had one.

Of course it was highly irregular for Wolfe to upstage the defense attorney and cross-examine the witness, Assistant District Attorney Perry Benjamin, but when the question came up, Claridge the prosecutor did not object. Why would he? The thought that a layman, a legal neophyte (so I imagine he judged Wolfe) would undertake a critical cross-examination that Golzer should have done must have delighted him.

Wolfe began by asking Perry Benjamin to describe the room they were in when he and Cramer were questioning Jack Gainslee.

"It was small. Smallish."

"Could you estimate its dimensions?"

"Maybe fifteen feet long by five or six wide."

"I assume it contained furniture?"

"Yes. A table and four chairs—wooden. A metal filing cabinet."

I wondered why Wolfe was wasting time on what I was sure were inconsequential details. I asked him about it afterward and he told me he meant to lull the witness with "meaningless minutiae." It was all a seemingly innocent prelude to a heads-on attack.

"The table," Wolfe prompted. "How big?"

Benjamin shrugged. "Not sure. I'll guess it's eight feet long and two feet wide—no, a little less. Why?"

"Why?" Wolfe echoed.

"Well, Mr. Wolfe, I know you're not a lawyer, but you've had wide experience of many aspects of the law. I just can't see that any of what you're asking is the least bit important."

"You're right, of course. Were there any objects on the table? Such as a gun?"

A decisive shake of Benjamin's head. "No. Why would there be?" He was beginning to sound both confused and perhaps a little worried. "The only things on the table were my notes, Inspector Cramer's notes, and a few glasses and a pitcher of water."

I saw him glance to the back of the courtroom. I turned and saw Belinda standing near the double doors.

"Very well," said Wolfe. "We're nearly done. But let me ask you this—I'm told you left the room to go to the rest room?"

"I did."

"Before you did so, did you at any time notice Inspector Cramer's weapon?"

"I did not. And I want to say that in my opinion, he is wholly innocent of the crime."

"Thank you for that generous assessment. Coming from you, it holds considerable weight. But, oh, I should have asked you this earlier—before you entered that small—smallish—room, as you put it, had you ever met the victim Jack Gainslee?"

"Well, of course I did! I was there when he was arrested."

Wolfe bestowed a beatific smile on him, then turned to the judge. "Your Honor, I am about to ask something that I expect will appear to have no relevance to these proceedings."

Her Lovelyship considered it and then beckoned him forward, as well as the prosecutor and the ostensible defense attorney. They back-and-forthed for a short time, none of which I heard, then they all resumed their respective places and Wolfe confronted the witness.

"Mr. Benjamin," he said, "do you have any siblings?"

Utter silence.

"Did you hear me, sir?"

A sound rather like a cough. "Yes."

"Yes, you heard me or yes, you have siblings?"

Another cough. "Both."

"Brothers? Sisters?"

"One sister."

"Is she in court today?"

Another silence and it was quite long, but Wolfe waited it out. Perry Benjamin finally stood up. "Go ahead," he said. "Book me. I killed him."

Which is the only time I ever saw in real life a situation that happened again and again on those old Perry Mason shows.

✗   ✗   ✗   ✗

You've worked it out, of course. Perry Benjamin is Ms. Belinda's brother. When he saw his opportunity, he sapped Cramer (reluctantly), grabbed his gun in a gloved hand and shot Jack Gainslee.

I'm glad to tell you that he got as light a sentence as possible under the circumstances.

But I'm sorry to say that I never got to meet Judge (Mary Tyler) Grove.

⚹   ⚹   ⚹   ⚹

A few nights after the trial, Inspector Cramer and Purley Stebbins arrived for dinner in the old brownstone on West 35th Street. Both were elegantly dressed and Purley thankfully ditched that silly bowtie.

Dinner was splendid. In the office afterward we enjoyed post prandials. Cramer finally broke the silence. "Wolfe, I don't know how to tell you how much I—"

My boss held up a forestalling hand. "No need, Inspector. I myself am at an uncustomary dearth of words."

Cramer nodded. "OK. But I've got to pay you something!"

"No. Sergeant Stebbins did that."

"He gave you one buck!"

"Yes, he did. But if I were to tally up my services in this affair, Inspector, I ought to pay *you*." Another upraised forestalling hand. "No, hear me out. Defending you afforded me great pleasure."

"I don't get it," Cramer grunted after draining his beer glass. "We've never been bosom buddies."

"Indisputable," said Wolfe, "yet I admire you, sir, for two reasons. You are a totally honest policeman. And even more important to me, you are no Gregson or Lestrade. Your mind is usually up to seeing things as they are and finding ways to fix them. Archie here even wrote up your own "Red Threads" case!"

Cramer thought it over for a while and then declared, "All right, then, *Nero*—" (In case you don't know, the last person to call him by his first name was his boyhood friend Marko Vukcic). "Nero, you're a big pain in the ass, but damn it, man, you're *my* pain and there have been a few occasions like now when I've really liked and admired you and if you ever remind me that I said this—*any of you!*—I'll kick your butts from here to the moon and back! Amen!" And he sat down, his face flushed, his eyes flashing like headlights, but the biggest smile on his puss that I've ever seen.

But it didn't last long. "Wolfe," he said—*bye-bye, Nero!*— "what's this goddam favor that I owe you?!"

"Just this. The next time that our professional paths cross and I tell you what I have or haven't done or thought, you will not call me a liar, but you will accept whatever I've told you as the truth. And I only ask this *once*, sir!"

Cramer looked sick. "That's *three* times too much!"

"Do I have your word?"

"If I bankrupt myself, I could pay you four thousand—"

"*Do* I have your word?"

With remarkable restraint, Cramer nodded, though he did add, "You can have *two* words, but I'll observe the niceties and not pronounce that one."

I tried to see him and Purley out, but they were gone before I got there, but I'll give Cramer this—

He did not slam the door.

✗

Marvin Kaye is the author of seventeen novels and numerous short stories, as well as the editor of best-selling anthologies, *Sherlock Holmes Mystery Magazine*, and *Weird Tales* magazine. A native of Philadelphia, he is a graduate of Penn State, with an M.A. in theatre and English literature.

THE SHED

by Ellen Wight

There were a few things that I came to learn about my husband in the ten years we were married. Martin was a good provider. Martin was a decent husband. Martin was thoughtful and well-liked by most people. He was a gentle soul with a kind nature. Martin was also a serial killer.

I came to suspect the last by a series of events that happened over the course of a month. As I think about it now, were there things I should have noticed along the way in the years we were together? Honestly speaking, I can say no. But having lived through the last month, I now have to live with the fact that I have spent the last decade of my life with a murderer. I also know for sure that his transformation had something to do with the shed.

For our tenth wedding anniversary, Martin "surprised" me with a cabin in the woods in the middle of nowhere. We are both city dwellers and love everything to do with what the city offers. I was a little surprised by his gift, but easily believed him when he told me he wanted to have time away from the pressures of the city and the remote cabin in the woods was exactly what we needed to get back to nature. We were both able to take a much-needed vacation from our jobs, so a few weeks in the woods seemed like a nice idea.

"Kay, this is exactly what we need to get grounded again … a new beginning."

He had such a hopeful look about him that I didn't have the heart to tell him that roughing it in the woods for the next few weeks was the last thing in the world that I wanted.

"The property is on twenty-five acres, including the house, and out back is the greatest shed that I can use for my workshop." Martin was a salesman by profession, but loved working with tools of any kind. His enthusiasm was catching and before long, we both looked forward to our getaway.

My enthusiasm died a quick death when I saw the cabin for the first time. It was in rough shape with a sagging porch and shingles and a roof that should have been replaced long ago. The broken shutters gave it a neglected look and the "burned wood" exterior made the house look as if someone had tried to set fire to it. We had to fetch water from a well, and the inside was as in need of repair as the outside. As horrified as I was, I thought it odd that Martin almost seemed gleeful and totally relaxed in this atmosphere. This was a man who at home needed 900 channels on the flat screen to be content.

"Kay, come look at the shed! Have you seen the shed?"

As I stood on the sagging porch, careful of my footing, I saw a large shed about fifty feet into a clearing. My first thought was that it was not only an odd place for a shed, but also the structure looked newer and in better shape than the cabin. It was painted red and while weather beaten, it was still in one piece and in pretty decent shape. Why would someone let their house fall apart and yet keep up the maintenance on a shed? The shed was about half the length of the cabin with a small section that looked like it was added on.

"Wow, that does look like it would make a terrific workshop. I'm happy for you, Martin."

"I'm happy for us! We can relax and reconnect here. No distractions from the city. I feel better already."

He felt better and I felt sick to my stomach, but I decided to make the best of it and plastered on a smile.

✗   ✗   ✗   ✗

Our first week there was spent fixing up what we could and making lists for the things we couldn't. The daytime was busy for both of us, but it was at night that I began to feel that something wasn't quite right.

First of all, Martin began spending a great deal of time in the shed. When we finally got out there to inspect it, there wasn't much to see. The former owners, the ones Martin wouldn't tell me about, had left the shed almost empty. What was my husband doing in there for hours when the only thing in there was a rusted chair and broken-down workbench? And yet night after night he spent time sweeping it out and just making plans for the "workshop" he was going to create. Oh, by the way, he told me that it was his "private" place and when he was working in the shed, I was to respect his privacy and stay away.

One evening, when we had been there about a week, I decided to sneak out to the shed and see what he was doing. Privacy was one thing, but my curiosity was starting to work on my nerves. I waited until it was dark and Martin had been out there for about an hour. The weather had been dry and so I had to walk slowly and carefully so as not to be heard. I couldn't take a flashlight because I didn't want Martin to see me. With the light from the full moon I crept along the path, occasionally spooked from the sounds of the woods around me.

When I finally reached the outer portion of the shed, I balanced myself on a piece of broken concrete and stood on my toes to glance into the grimy back window. At first I saw nothing but blackness and thought the shed was empty. Then, as I was about to turn away, I saw a slight movement. As my eyes grew accustomed to the dark, I could make out Martin's form, sitting in the chair with his hands behind the back of the chair like they were tied behind him.

He stared at the floor almost like he was asleep while humming the same note over and over to himself and rocking his body back and forth. I was so taken aback by what I saw that I almost fell backwards off the ledge that I was leaning on. I couldn't wrap my mind around the fact that I now had the answer to my question. He was doing nothing in the shed but staring at a portion of the floor and rocking … for hours at a time, in almost a catatonic state. What was going on? And the bigger question was, what was I going to do about it?

✗   ✗   ✗   ✗

The next week brought unexpected changes. Martin made a number of trips to town, which by the way, was ten miles away. The feeling of isolation made the cabin seem like it existed by itself, but an active town was in reality only fifteen minutes out.

He told me he bought a few power tools and a new workbench to start his woodworking projects. As I worked in the kitchen, the sounds of a power saw and drill could be constantly heard and that made me feel better. Day and night he escaped to the shed to work.

Maybe the other night was just an off night for him and now he would be focused on his woodworking and everything would go back to normal. I was wrong.

During one of his frequent trips to town, I decided to spy again and see what he accomplished while working in the shed. As he left he seemed distracted and distant, but I chalked that up to the adjustment from city life to the woods. During the day the trip through the clearing was much faster and easier, but to my shock, the door to the shed was padlocked! Was he trying to keep intruders out, or keep me out?

I climbed again on the broken ledge and glanced through the grimy back window. The room was empty. I blinked a few times because I knew I'd been listening to power tools day and night. The rusted chair remained in the middle of the room and the broken table in the corner. Where was the equipment that I had been listening to? And why lock an empty room? What was this place, and why was my husband changing right before my eyes?

I've always criticized characters in movies who had mysterious things happen around them, and yet they remained where they were. How stupid could you be? But now, with a real mystery on my hands, I understood why the characters wanted to stay.

I needed to know and understand what was happening in the shed. I couldn't go back without knowing.

Confronting Martin would have been a waste of time. He was guarded and defensive any time the subject of the shed was brought up. Maybe I would take a trip to town to see if I could locate and talk to the original owners of the property. Had they experienced anything unusual? What was the history of the property? I wasn't even sure if there were records anywhere, but Martin had to have bought the property from someone.

Week three found me searching for public records of the sale of the property. Late one afternoon at the small town hall, I found a clerk of public records who was willing to help me. I didn't give my name, but decided to ask a general question about the previous owner of the cabin.

"Sorry, ma'am. That property that you're talking about hasn't been bought or sold for a long time. Are you sure about the address? According to these records, this here fella has owned the property for going on twenty years."

"Any mention of a shed on the property?" I asked in a whisper.

"By golly, yeah! Seems it's built over an old abandoned well that probably dried up and died years ago. Why? I'm sure that well would be no use to anyone today." He pointed a stubby finger at the name on the deed to my cabin. My husband's name. He had owned the property for decades.

So many thoughts were tumbling through my head on the way home. Why had he lied to me about the cabin and the shed? Why the whole "surprise" idea? One thought kept running through my mind: he's hiding something. The time had come to find out his secret. By this time it was dark and raining heavily, but I didn't care. Tonight I would force Martin to tell me the whole truth.

Between the inky dark and the rain I could barely make out the shed, but I was fueled by my anger, so my quick strides got me there in a flash. I went right up to the door and banged my fists on it, screaming Martin's name.

The door opened so suddenly I almost fell backwards.

"I've been waiting for you, Kay."

I walked inside and he closed the door behind me. The only light was from a lantern, and I couldn't see his eyes clearly in the dimness, but the Martin I knew was gone. I was afraid of the man standing before me.

"Martin, what's going on? We need to talk. Now."

His laugh was low and terrifying. "I didn't want to make such an unpleasant decision, but it's time for you to join the others. You should have minded your own business, Kay."

I backed away. "Martin, I don't understand. What others?" My eyes adjusted to the lantern light. Behind him, a huge hole gaped in the floor—the opening to the abandoned well.

"The ones just like you. Would you believe that one of them tried to burn the house down? I corrected her the way I corrected all the others. Now it's time to correct you."

My heart hammered. He was going to throw me into the well, just like he did the others. I had to keep him talking.

"Martin, did you hurt other women?"

"They forced me to," he spat. "They all interfered with my time here, like you did. Now you'll end up like them. Don't worry, though. I'll visit you, just like I visit them."

My time was running out.

He approached me, his back to the well. I swung around and grabbed the rusted chair, thrusting it at his middle with all my might. He lost his balance and stepped backwards into the hole, his hands reaching, clutching at the chair, at me. I'm not sure if he was trying to regain his balance or attempting to pull me into the well with him, but he couldn't reach me.

He fell, screaming, into the well. It's a scream I will remember until the day I die.

And then there was silence.

✗   ✗   ✗   ✗

The police helped put all the pieces together. Martin had been luring young women to the cabin for years. The well contained the remains of a least four victims, which coincided with missing person reports throughout the years. He used the abandoned well as a burial ground for his victims. The well was concealed by a wooden trapdoor, which was almost undetectable. The shed helped him cover his sins.

It's been six months since the tragedy, and in that time I had the cabin and the shed completely leveled. Nothing remains of those structures. I gave the land to the county. I wasn't going to profit from Martin's activities. Even though, as his wife, I was entitled to the land, I walked away from it forever.

As I look to the future, I cannot help but feel imprisoned by the past. I take things day by day, trying to move forward with my life.

Today I received a letter from the town, thanking me for the gracious gift of the land. They had decided to sell the land and already had a buyer. The profit would be used to make county improvements. I skimmed the letter quickly, but the last two sentences made my blood run cold.

"While the homeowners are thrilled with the land that they will build upon, they do have one question. Do you have the key to the padlock on the door of the large shed that's in the clearing behind where the house used to be?"

✗

Ellen Wight is originally from Brooklyn, New York, but has resided in New Hampshire for the last twenty-eight years where she lives with her husband, three children and five pets. She currently works as a reading specialist for an elementary school. Reading mysteries has always been a favorite pastime of hers and she finds she loves writing them as well.

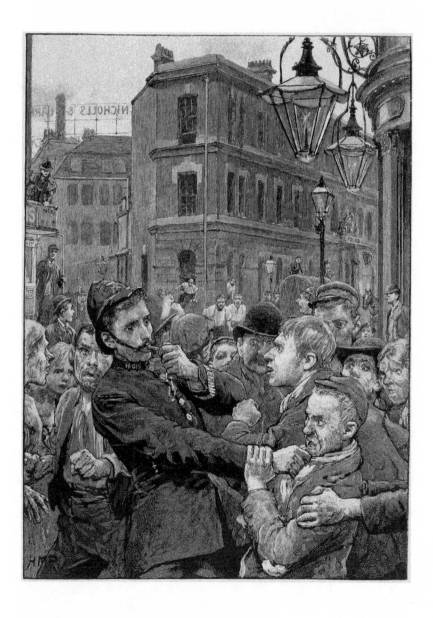

CAREER TRANSITIONS

by Marian McMahon Stanley

Jimmy aggravated the wrong people by saying too much to certain parties he shouldn't have even been talking to. You can't let those things pass. Even somebody with bricks for brains like Jimmy Scanlan knows that.

So Jimmy decides to go into his own witness protection program and disappear for a while. Now our Jimmy is a magna cum laude graduate of the School of Stupid, so it doesn't take long for him to screw up.

Jimmy's favorite uncle dies in Queens. We wait. A gorgeous flower arrangement arrives—Asiatic lilies, long-stemmed white roses, purple irises—the whole nine yards. No name, but it's not hard to track the florist down to a little town outside of Binghamton.

⚹   ⚹   ⚹   ⚹

Ruggiero Blandini here—Richie the Iceman for short. Not too many people know my real name. I use lots of names. I'm what you might call a problem solver. Anyway, next day, I'm in Vestal, New York, driving past a little ranch with a black Caddy SUV sitting in the carport. Like I said, School of Stupid. He couldn't bring himself to lie low and drive a dark-colored Honda Civic or a Corolla. No, it had to be a black Caddy SUV. Oh yeah, with tinted windows.

I watch Jimmy for a couple of days. I can tell he's getting comfortable. He comes out to do his errands, mow the lawn, take the damned car to the carwash, whatever. So after a while I'm getting restless and decide to get the job done.

Late afternoon of the second day, Jimmy drives into Binghamton, eats an early dinner at the Lost Dog Café on Water Street and stops at the CVS on Main afterwards. I watch for him from the car I'm using for this job—an old black Subaru emancipated a few days before from a student parking area in Syracuse. It's dinner time for most people in Binghamton and the CVS parking lot is all but empty, a satisfying lull in customer traffic.

Jimmy does his shopping and comes out the door. He's so relaxed now in his own little witness protection program that he's not even looking around to check the lot. Some people make my job easy.

One clean shot and he drops like a bag of turnips. I put the Glock back in its special black gym bag and take my leave out the back exit of the parking lot. Last time I see Jimmy Scanlan, he's lying on the blacktop, still holding a white plastic CVS bag with his hemorrhoid medicine in one hand and his black Caddy SUV car keys in the other.

I drop the Subaru on a small side street, pick up my own gray Acura on the same street, and head west out of Binghamton on Route 17. Somewhere between Olean and Jamestown, I pull off and find the bed and breakfast I'd looked up on the New York State Visitors Bureau website. I told the lady at the bed and breakfast that I'd be late. She said not to worry, that she'd leave the key under the mat and that she might be up working, anyway. That's what I like about these places. Homey.

I like to stay at bed and breakfasts when I'm on the road. Old farmhouses or Victorians with wraparound porches. Blueberry pancakes, homemade muffins, and strong coffee served at a heavy round table in an old-fashioned dining room. If I ever retire—and God knows, I have enough stashed away in the Caymans I could do that any time now—I'd open a place myself somewhere upstate. I make a nice breakfast frittata and I use a touch of cardamom in my yogurt fruit salad. I like to make things a little different.

When I stay at these places, I pay in cash and give some random name. If they ask, I tell them I'm in logistics for a metal fastener company in Sandusky, Michigan, or something like that. Nobody ever asks you inconvenient questions about logistics or metal fasteners. You can see their eyes glaze over as soon as the words are out of your mouth. And that's good.

I'm the only guest and that's good, too. Quiet. Lately I need to rest a little between jobs. The house is a fine old Victorian. Nice location—on the main street across from the library in a little town near a state reservation, not too far off the highway.

The minute I pull into the driveway, even in the dark I can see this is a class job. When I turn the key and open the front door, I'm blown away. Original woodwork, beading on the wooden railings curving up the stairway, stained glass to die for—you should pardon the expression. The smell of strawberry-rhubarb muffins just cooked and coffee perking. My dreams fulfilled.

Rita, the innkeeper, comes out of the kitchen. Behind her, I can see an open laptop surrounded by stacks of paper on a green granite counter. Rita's an older woman wearing a light blue sweat suit, no wedding ring, and a spiked hairstyle that looks kind of funny on her. She pours me a cup of decaf coffee and hands me a hot muffin. "I thought you might need something after your drive. Where're you coming from again—Cleveland?"

"Yeah, Cleveland. Thanks. This is terrific. And this place—gorgeous."

I can see Rita is pleased and she offers to give me a tour even though it's late. I love the fact that she invites me to take my coffee and muffin with me as we walk and talk. Rita's spent the past five years painstakingly renovating the house. And, boy, could you see the quality of the work. My soul is nourished just by walking room to room. I feel like I'm in a cathedral—like Chartres or something. I'd like to wake up in a place like this every day.

I'm not surprised to find that Rita is a great cook. It's a disappointment that she talks so much—nonstop. But still, I like to hear about the renovations of old houses. You know, it might come in handy if I ever I open a place of my own.

✗   ✗   ✗   ✗

The next morning over breakfast, our conversation gets a little more complicated when I ask her again just when she'd bought the place.

"Well," she says, after a short pause. "Actually, I couldn't afford the down payment at the time, so I did a lease to buy." Then her wrinkly face starts to get red and I know that Rita has some sad story, that I'm going to hear the sad story and that she's probably going to cry on me. Shit. I hate it when they cry.

"The house was just a wreck. It was on the market for years. No one wanted to tackle it until I came along." Rita takes a deep, shaky breath to try to calm herself. "Sorry." She starts to cry, anyway.

"That's okay," I say. But it's really not okay. I hate it when they cry. I can feel the beginnings of a headache just above my left eye.

"So now the lease is up. The owner wants to sell this place for three times what it was worth when I found it. I could never afford that." It's hard to understand what Rita is saying now, because she is starting to blubber. I hate blubbering. "And the only reason it's worth that much is because of all the work I put into it."

"Did he pay for any of the work, Rita?" She shakes her head.

"Did he know you were doing the work?"

She nods. "He did, but now," here Rita wails, "now he says that he never really gave me permission to do any of this work and he's going to evict me if I can't make an offer for the house at the new price by the end of the month. It's like he just played me, used me, working so hard to fix the house up. I'm such a fool."

Oh, Christ. My spirit doesn't feel so nourished now.

"No lawyer when you did the original agreement?"

"I guess I didn't have a very good one." She's getting quieter, sniffling and reaching into her sweat suit sleeve for a hidden tissue. "My divorce just went through, and I was trying to make a new start."

I brace myself for more tears, but Rita holds it together. "He wouldn't have given me permission to do all this work or spend any money. Some old aunt left the house to him. He didn't care about it. Never comes out. Lives somewhere around Boston. Calls it the sticks here."

She pauses, and her lower lip trembles. I think we might hit the waterworks again. "And now, he wants to make money off of all my work and evict me." Rita raises a shaking hand and covers her eyes. "Oh, I'm so sorry to be telling you all my personal troubles." She makes an effort, straightens her shoulders and stands to clear the table. "I'll just get some of this out of the way." She gives me a watery smile. "You want a second cup of coffee?"

After breakfast I go to my room—the Jade Room. Rita had named all the rooms—kind of corny, but I like it. The Jade Room is all in greens—mostly soft tones. There's a bay window with one of those wide window seats—very comfortable. I'll have to remember that for when I open my own place.

I sit on the window seat and look around before I place my hands on my knees, breathe deeply and close my eyes to meditate.

You need to keep yourself centered in a job like mine. I like to stay centered.

✗   ✗   ✗   ✗

Half an hour later, I check my Cayman accounts again. Plenty of cushion. Too much. I always told myself that when I got to a certain amount, I'd check out of this business. It can be stressful, and how long can a guy stay lucky? I blew past that certain amount in the bank account years ago.

I think about it and decide it's my ego. I'm in high demand because I have what you'd call a unique skill set and a sure hand. I solve problems nice and clean, in and out, no trace, no fuss. Hardly anybody knows my real name. Hell, I don't even remember it half the time. The jobs seem too easy right now. Every once in a while, I think I'd like to take a few really risky assignments—just to show myself how good I am. That's the ego. Me and Jimmy Scanlan, graduates of the School of Stupid.

My next work commitment is a tragic accident that I need to schedule for an investment banker who spends summer weekends at a big house in the Hamptons. The guy was supposed just to be doing the laundry for my clients, but he got in the habit of skimming off the top—see aforementioned big house in the Hamptons. Easy job to pull off—road accident on a winding road late at night.

I have a short break before that one. I can fit in a little business of my own before I take my ride to the Hamptons. And then after the Hamptons I might close shop. It's a little scary for me to think about that. They say it's good to phase into retirement so that you don't go off a cliff. That might be a challenge in my line of work. But I'm thinking that if I plan it right—go toward something, you know, instead of just leaving something behind, I'll be okay. I'm a good planner.

✗   ✗   ✗   ✗

I head to Boston right after I leave Rita's place. It's not too hard to find the hotshot who owns Rita's house and wants to take advantage of a hard-working, if naïve, woman of a certain age who's on her own. Hot Shot's name is Betts. He works at some kind of venture capital firm and has a nice spread in a desirable suburb. There's a basketball hoop set on the house's three car garage that never gets used—the hoop, that is, not the garage. Cute blond wife in yoga pants hopping in and out of a BMW SUV. Tight stressed face. What gives? Isn't she living the life in Perfectville? Don't see any sign of kids. Maybe they go to boarding school.

Betts works out at a toney gym in the financial district. He's buff. Everyone in there is buff. There might as well be a sign on the door, "No body fat allowed." Betts goes to the early morning spinning class. There are some fine-looking young women in that early morning spinning class. Betts likes one in particular. He leans against the wall with one arm and watches while she does her stretches. They've got something going. That's helpful.

Ms. Hot Spinner lives in a brownstone apartment in the South End. That's convenient, not too far from the Southeast Expressway, the route Betts uses to drive home after a late-night business meeting in the brownstone apartment with spinner lady.

So I wait for Betts in a little park across the street one night while he's having his hot meeting with the lady in the brownstone. The well-tended, nice little park is one of those that are locked and reserved just for residents. As if. I learned all I needed to know about popping locks from my Uncle Sammy when I was twelve. Less than ten seconds for this one.

After a long while, Betts comes down the stairs and when he reaches the sidewalk, turns to wave and blow a kiss up to the second floor. Sweet. I meet him a half a block up. Neighborhood's quiet. I'm leaning against his Mini Cooper.

A frown crosses Betts's face. Wait, somebody's leaning on his car. *Somebody's leaning on his car.* "Get off my car," he says.

I smile. I stand. Did I tell you that I'm a big man? You don't have to be big to do what I do—the little guys are usually much meaner—but sometimes it helps. I don't say anything. I just hit him twice quick—once in his well-toned abs and once on his handsome square jaw. He drops and sits on the sidewalk, gripping his gut and moaning.

He fumbles for his wallet and his car keys. "Take the car. Take the money," he croaks.

"I don't want your money or tweety little car. I spit on your tweety little car. Get up."

"I can't," he whimpers, sounding like a little girl, drawing it out "*I c-aaa-n-'t.*"

Oh, please.

"Oh, Christ. Yes, you can." He flinches and cries a little when I put my arm around him and half-drag him to the park. I shake my head and exchange smiles with a young guy who comes around the corner with a Northeastern backpack. "Never could hold his booze. Never learns." My hand is squeezing Betts's right shoulder enough so that he knows not to do anything stupid.

Betts tries to pull back when we get to the park, now darkened since I disabled the cute period lights by the pathway. "What are you going to do to me?" he gasps in that high, squeaky kind of voice.

"Nothing you can't handle. If you do what I say."

So Mr. Betts and I have a serious business discussion about the price point for the house his aunt left him. This discussion is punctuated by a couple of quick jabs to the side of the head when Mr. Betts has the erroneous impression that we are in a conference room on State Street and that he's actually in a negotiation instead of being in a dark city park with a very dangerous man and in a conversation where there is only one right answer.

Betts limps back to his tweety little car after we have an understanding about what the sale contract is going to say and when he will get the sale completed. Week's end is good or he'll get another visit. We, of course, also discuss the standard fine print clause of our own agreement—the part that talks about what will happen to Mr. Betts if he should contact the authorities. I'm pretty sure he's not that stupid.

⚡   ⚡   ⚡   ⚡

The next week I call Rita about my favorite navy-blue cardigan that I might have left at her bed and breakfast. I hate cardigans and I never wear navy blue, but whatever. Rita starts to talk so fast after she answers the call that she can hardly breathe—telling me all about Mr. Betts's sudden change of heart.

"You know, he must have thought about things and decided it's better to be fair. Do you think he went to church?"

"Well, there you are, Rita. I'll bet he had a talk with his priest. Anyway, that's good news. I'm happy for you." I listen some more and some more again—I told you how much she talked, right?—before I get around to trying to close the call. "So you didn't see the sweater? Well, I guess I must have left it somewhere else."

"No, I'm sorry, I didn't. I'd tell you to stop by when you're in the area again, but I'm thinking that since Mr. Betts gave me such a good deal, I might sell out myself if I can get that higher price, too. I'm not getting any younger and this is a big place to manage. With that money I could get a nice condo down near my daughter in Jersey and still have a good retirement fund."

I'm surprised, but not too much. "Oh, no kidding, Rita. Well, it is a big place and you deserve a reward for all your hard work."

"You're so sweet to say so. Hey, if you give me your address, I can send you your sweater if it shows up."

"Oh, that's okay. I suppose it's in the back of the car or in the hall closet." And I finally manage to say my goodbyes. Nice woman, but—Jesus—she can go on.

✗   ✗   ✗   ✗

The Hamptons job is quick and easy. It's a real tragedy—a pillar of the community cut down in the prime of life when his car spins off the road late at night. It's a shame, but it happens.

The next morning I call my contacts and tell them I'm out of the business for good. They complain and start talking about some lucrative jobs they have on the line for me. I hang up. I cancel all communication—the post office box, the phone number that my agent Joey at the variety store uses to call me about a job, everything. By the end of the morning, I'm totally disappeared. Just the way I like it.

I make the next call on my new cell phone under my new name—Harrison Judge. Like it? I thought it had some class—a certain gravitas. Anyway, my next call is to a realty office in western New York with the listing for a Victorian Bed and Breakfast somewhere between Olean and Jamestown.

While I'm waiting for the receptionist to get the listing agent on the line, I think about how I'll extend the gardens out back of Rita's place. Maybe put in a gazebo where guests can enjoy an iced tea in the summer. People like little touches like that, you know.

✗

Marian McMahon Stanley is the author of two Rosaria O'Reilly mysteries from Barking Rain Press: *The Immaculate* (May 2016) and *Buried Troubles* (May 2018). She enjoyed a long international corporate career and, most recently, a senior position at a large urban university. Marian writes in a small town outside Boston.

THE OCCURRENCE OF THE MARCHING MARIONETTE

A DR. ARGENT MYSTERY

by Teel James Glenn

Lady Camden woke with a start and a sense that something was very wrong. Her first reaction was to reach for her husband for re-assurance but there was only an empty space beside her on the bed.

"Jason," she whispered aloud as she remembered he was not there, that he would never be there again, dead these three months. "Jason," she repeated in a minor key. "How will I live without you?"

She was aware then of a low, muffled sound, like a wind rustling trees or the sound of waves against a distant shore. She reached over to light the lamp by her bed and peered into the darkness of her bedroom.

It was as it had always been, her sanctuary for thirty years of marriage: dressers, armoire, chairs, and the wide hearth above which the wedding portrait of she and her husband hung.

She sat up.

The whispering noise persisted, now more insistent and regular. It was a voice, barely audible and it spoke one word.

"Camilla!" it said.

Her name.

"Who, who is there?" she said.

She pulled on a dressing gown and thrust her feet into slippers before grasping her cane in one hand and the table lamp in another.

"Camilla!" the voice came again, this time clearly from the hallway.

Lady Camden made her way slowly across the room, restrain-ing herself from the impulse to call out to her maid for fear the sounds were only her imaginings. After all, who would call to her in the empty house in the middle of the night, using her Christian name?

It was only she and Regina, her maid, in the main house, the butler being away to his sister's for a family emergency. All the other help lived off premises; her late husband had insisted on it to give him privacy with his work.

She looked over at the shelves of the bookcase that stood beside the hearth where some of her husband's work, his other passion, sat. Marionettes.

The late Lord Camden had been passionate about the carved wooden figures since childhood, a passion that predated his meeting and falling in love with his lady. From the first she accepted that she was, as she used to joke, 'mistress to the marionettes.'

In the flickering gaslight the tiny faces looked out at her with empty eyes; when her husband was alive they had always seemed warm and comforting, as if a conclave of family—but now they only reminded her that the sustaining love of her husband was gone.

Now the harlequins and ballerinas, knights and dragons sat without the spark of life her husband infused in them, both in the carving and in the performances he would put on for children. In a way, the wooden puppets had been the children they never had.

All that was past now, yet she had not the will to remove them, even at the recommendation of her friends, who said it was morbid to keep them around.

"Camilla!" the voice called again, this time distinctly from the other side of the door.

"What—what do you want?" she said haltingly. She was gripped with a sudden dread as she reached for the door handle, the cane in her hand making it a clumsy operation. "Who are you?"

In answer the hissed voice said, "Someone who cares, my flower."

She gasped. Only her husband ever called her "my flower," his pet name for her. Her hand felt palsied, frozen on the knob.

"Camilla," the whispered voice called.

She had to open the door, no matter how much she feared. Her hand shook.

She pulled the door inward and stepped out into the hall like someone deciding to jump into a cool pool of water all at once to ease the shock. She held her cane now like a cudgel, prepared for some cruel joke.

The gaslamps in the hall were high up, but focused down so that the ceiling was lost in blackness and the rest of the hall flickering in gloom. To the right were the stairs to the ground floor and Regina's rooms. To the left, the corridor to the west wing of the house and the staircase to her husband's attic workroom.

The whisper came from her left and she turned to face a horror such as she could never have imagined.

Far down the corridor there was movement.

"Who is there?" Lady Camden called shrilly. "Who are you—"

The words stuck in her throat as she saw just who—or what—was in the corridor.

At first she had thought it was someone, a soldier in full uniform, far down the hallway, barely illuminated by the lamp she held. Then she realized the movement was much closer. In fact, the figure that moved toward her with an awkward rolling marching step was small.

Too small to be human.

"No!" she gasped.

The figure was a marionette in full Horseguard uniform!

"Camilla, my flower!" the whispered voice came again.

"No!" Her Ladyship yelled, "No!" But her words had no effect on the oddly ambling, brightly painted figure as it progressed down the hallway toward her with a slow, steady, bobbing pace.

She backed up, her hands trembling so badly that she was in danger of dropping her lamp. She pointed the cane at the apparition like a sword, the brass tip wavering with her palsied hand.

"Ma'am?" A female voice caused Lady Camden to whirl so that she almost struck her maid with the out-flung cane.

"Regina!"

Her Ladyship all but collapsed against her maid, letting the cane drop, and she held onto the girl for a moment, burying her face in the girl's shoulder.

"What it is, ma'am?" the maid asked.

There was a hissing sound and Her Ladyship cried, "There!" and turned back to point at the apparition. The marionette was no longer walking. "It was Jason come back for me, I know it."

"What, ma'am?" the maid asked with genuine confusion. "It is only an old puppet."

Indeed, the wooden figure lay in a tangled pile in the center of the hallway, the control board atop it, as lifeless as a dead thing.

✗   ✗   ✗   ✗

"And those are the facts as I know them, Doctor," the detective inspector said as he completed his recitation and looked up from his notes. "As Lady Camden and her maid, a Miss Regina Franchi, related them to me."

Dr. Augustus Argent nodded, his features a mask of concentration. He was tall and thin, with long, white hair and narrow, strong features. He had white mustachios and spade beard, and with his somewhat old-fashioned long coat, looked like a hero from one of those Frontier American Penny Dreadfuls. He was, however, Minister Without Portfolio for the Crown concerning Occult Affairs.

"I suspect you were thorough in your questionings, Inspector Lestrade?" my mentor and employer said with no challenge in his tone.

The detective inspector was sallow and somewhat rat-faced, with dark eyes which blinked frequently. "I know your methods, sir," he said, his long hands making quick and energetic gestures. "And have done my best to be thorough."

"No doubt," Dr. Argent said with a genial smile. "I have noted that in our past interactions."

On that cold spring day we were sitting in the common room of the Guv's Carnaby Street office-home—a converted stable. I had been completing my notes on the ghastly business of the Pinchion Street Occurrence when the detective inspector came to consult us.

"Most interesting, Lestrade," Dr. Argent said as he rose. He paced across the room with the long-legged grace of a dancer. "I suspect the Baker Street fellow might also be interested in this—"

"I thought of that, sir," Lestrade said, "but he is off to Reigate on a case and you are, after all, so very close."

"Well, we shall not feel slighted in being on the B team then," the Guv joked.

"There is more, of course, Doctor," the inspector continued.

"I suspected as much," my employer and mentor said. "Pray continue."

"I had been called previously to investigate Lord Camden's accident."

"Accident? Could you elaborate?"

"Cut and dried, actually, sir," Lestrade said. "Their maid found Lord Camden at the foot of the main stairs after a late-night fall. I investigated, and it was just a tragic accident, nothing suspicious at all."

"So how does this relate to the occurrence of the marionette?"

"I returned to the house with a constable the following day, both to complete my report and see how Her Ladyship was faring," Lestrade continued. "I was met by the maid and found that Her Ladyship was resting, given a sedative by her doctor. Regina went into the bedroom ahead of me to awaken her mistress. Not five minutes went by when she yelled for us and we raced in.

"Our eyes were drawn to where the two women were staring at the walls and ceiling of the room, where in the flickering gaslight, there were a series of marks. At first glance the small marks appeared to be miniature footprints!

"These prints appeared to march in echelon up the wall, across the low ceiling and directly to the hearth shelf, where rows of marionettes sat at silent attention.

"I moved swiftly to the wall and set about examining the marks, which I now saw were indeed parallel prints, but one was of a small shoe and the other a round black smudge.

"I found my attention drawn to the shelf with the marionettes. One particular figure drew my scrutiny, a peg-legged pirate. The pattern on the wall was now clear; one shoe and one peg-leg marked a path along the wall."

"And I can assume that the marks were soot?" Dr. Argent said.

"Yes, Doctor," the policeman said. "Chimney soot."

"I see no direct reason for Scotland Yard to be called in," I said, interrupting the conversation for the first time. "Since no crime has been committed, Inspector, why are you involved?"

The Yard man assumed a meek posture and shook his head. "It is true, Captain, that there was no crime as such—perhaps some ghostly doings to interest the Doctor here, or at worst a prank—but Lady Camden's husband, dead these three months, was a stand-up chap. Gave shows with his puppets for the children at the orphanage and such before his accident. She is a great lady and if we can give her comfort—"

The Guv put a hand on the policeman's shoulder. "Why, Lestrade, you are in great danger of humanizing the long arm of the law with your feeling. Of course we will come; and we shall see if there might indeed be a crime here, eh?"

It was becoming a familiar routine, the unexpected call from the authorities and then a plunge into some exotic, horrifying escapade with Dr. Argent.

I had not realized how much I had become accustomed to it until I felt my pulse race when he said, "Looks like we are off to Camden House, Jack, to see this marching marionette for ourselves."

✗   ✗   ✗   ✗

The trip to Belgravia was a short trip by hansom.

Dr. Argent said nothing on the trip, his concentration absolute on what the detective inspector had reported. In no time at all we found ourselves outside the house, standing in a light drizzle. A bobbie stood guard out front and nodded to the inspector as he led us up the steps.

We were met inside by a small, dark-haired girl who was wringing her hands nervously.

"Inspector," she said in a shrill voice. "Can we leave now?"

"I am sorry, Miss Franchi," Lestrade said to her, "but until we have completed a thorough investigation we will need you on hand."

She looked at the doctor and me with hooded eyes, then said, "Her Ladyship is resting now, but she should leave this place," she said. "It has bad vibrations."

"Vibrations?" Dr. Argent asked.

"Ethereal vibrations. There are dark forces at work here."

"Really?" the Guv said. "And how do you know this?"

"I—I just know," she said.

"Franchi is a Corsican name, is it not?"

"What does that have to do with anything?" she asked with a sharp tone.

"I have been told that the people of that island have a greater sensitivity to such things than many others," my silver-haired mentor said.

"Just so," she said. "Just so."

"This is where Lord Camden died?" Dr. Argent asked as our group moved to the stairs.

"Yes, sir," the small girl said. She grimaced. "Terrible it was, him lying there, tangled in the strings of that horrible puppet he had been carrying."

"How did it happen?"

"It was late at night, sir," she said. "His Lordship often worked late. Walked the halls he did, to his workroom, which is why he had the other servants move out. And sometimes he would come down to the kitchen for a bite to eat. I guess he got distracted coming down the stairs. Or so the police said."

"It seems that way, Doctor," Lestrade said. "I investigated myself and there was nothing amiss."

"And you found him?" Argent asked her.

"Yes, sir. I heard an odd sort of cry—I was awake, reading in my room—and came out to investigate."

"I see," the Guv said noncommittally.

"Your mistress," the detective inspector asked. "Where is she?"

"In her room, sir," Regina said, "She does not leave it often, now; hoping, she says, for some other sign from His Lordship from beyond. I tried to get her to move to one of the other rooms or to leave this place altogether, but she would not have it."

"Is the constable still with her?" Lestrade asked.

"Outside her door, sir."

The girl led the three of us up the central staircase to the first floor corridor. The walls were hung with family portraits and the history of the Camdens was on full display.

The uniformed officer stood at the door of Lady Camden's room and came to attention when we came up the stairs.

"Anything further happen, Collins?" Lestrade asked.

"No, sir. I examined the room before Her Ladyship entered and all was normal." He looked down the darkened hallway to where a bright bundle sat in the center of the floor. "But I don't mind saying it's a little disturbing, with that thing down there."

"None of that," Lestrade chided him.

"I had better go in first," Regina said in a quiet voice, "to see that Her Ladyship is decent."

"Of course," Dr. Argent said.

The girl knocked and went inside, leaving the four of us in the hall.

"Nothing has been touched?" Dr. Argent walked down the hall toward the puppet that lay crumpled on the rug.

"Nothing, Doctor," the inspector said. "Once the word came to us I knew you would want a clear field."

"Well done," Argent said. He knelt to look at the wood-and-cloth marionette that mimicked a fallen soldier. He produced a magnifying glass and concentrated on the puppet for a few moments, and then on the floor around it. He produced a white handkerchief and daubed it in several places around the figure and on the wooden crosspiece that rested atop it that functioned as the controller.

When he rose, I could see a fine powder on the white cloth, but could not divine its significance. He then took a feather from an inner pocket of his jacket and tossed it in the air, watching with interest as it floated across the hall and eventually to the floor.

"This is becoming most interesting, Jack," he said to me. "I suspect Baker Street might have enjoyed this."

"All right, gentlemen," Regina called.

"Be alert, Lestrade," Dr. Argent said. "This might become quite unpleasant in a moment." He then turned and led the three of us into Her Ladyship's room, stopping in the doorway.

The maid stood by the bed, where a disheveled Lady Camden sat clutching the covers to her chest, her eyes showing a deep sadness.

The Guv walked across the room to the shelf, directly to the pirate marionette, and touched its shoe.

"It was Jason's favorite," Lady Camden said in a strained voice. "He used to love to enact *Treasure Island* for the children—and now he has come back to tell me something, I know he has."

"He wants you to leave this place," Regina spoke up. She stood beside the shattered lady and looked nervously at the shelf of marionettes.

"No such thing, madam," Dr. Argent said. He reached under the shelf and seemed to find something. Then he drew himself up to his full height, his piercing eyes boring into the maid's. "I have many reasons to believe in the survival of the consciousness, more than you can imagine. I have seen many examples of it; however, this is not one of them." He walked over to stand directly in front of the girl and loomed over her petite form.

"I will dismiss the fact that I feel no etheric emanations from this place," he said, "and confine myself to the prosaic clues made clear to me about this matter. One—while you were meticulous, Regina, in your attempts to make this all seem more than it is— even using powder to cover the piano-wire strings of the puppets to keep them from reflecting the lamplight. I found traces of the powder in the hall." He held out the kerchief smudged with the powder he had discovered in the corridor. "I noted that the lamps are so angled as to cast shadows upward, concealing the ceiling from any light … and to hide the means of transporting the puppets: helium balloons in black. I noted also that when the inspector recounted the initial incident, Her Ladyship was looking away at the moment she heard a hissing sound—I conjecture it was you using a blowgun or tube to puncture the balloon that allowed the puppet to 'walk.'"

The girl's expression showed extreme fear and she looked at the door.

I interposed myself between her and the door, standing next to the uniformed officer.

"You are mistaken, sir," Regina protested. "We—I saw that devil walking. And those—" She pointed to the prints on the wall. "How do you explain that? Obviously the spirit of—"

"Oh, tosh!" the Guv exclaimed. He held up a metal tube that he unfolded to a telescoping rod. "This is the explanation for that; it was secreted under the shelf—the only careless thing she has done in all this. She used this to create the fake footprints while Her Ladyship slept by putting soot on the end of it, using a small shoe for one foot and removing it for the 'peg-leg.' I am sure you will find the shoe in her room."

Lady Camden made a small, frightened noise, looking from Dr. Argent to her maid with pained confusion.

He continued, "If I had not suspected her earlier, finding this rod would be enough."

"Suspected her earlier?" I asked.

"The moment I saw the powder and the feather as it floated in the hallway, Jack. The air currents were just right for a balloon to make its way down the hall. And I noted that the lamps were curiously set to keep the ceiling in darkness, not at all the usual thing for even such a gloomy old townhouse."

"You are wrong, sir," Regina insisted in a plaintive voice. "I saw it. I didn't do anything wro—" Suddenly the woman bolted past Dr. Argent, straight at me and Collins.

The constable moved to stop her but abruptly yelled and fell back, a long slash on his neck from a knife the girl produced. I grabbed him as he fell, at the same time reaching out for her. The girl made it past me, and I took my scarf and threw it to the fallen officer to staunch the wound.

"Hold pressure on this, Collins," I yelled as I turned to race after her.

"Stop!" I made it out the door in time to see her reach the top of the stairs. She looked back at me with a mixture of fear and hatred in her expression. That was when she mis-stepped.

The girl's foot missed the top step and she went tumbling headlong down the staircase.

By the time I reached the top of the flight, it was over. At the bottom Regina Franchi lay still, her neck at an odd angle. She was dead.

When I returned to the room, Dr. Argent was already comforting Lady Camden.

"But I don't understand," Her Ladyship said when I informed them all that the girl was dead. "Why would she do such a thing?"

"And why run?" Lestrade asked. He was kneeling by his man and attending to Collins's wound. "As you stated before, Captain Stone, there has actually been no crime committed here."

"I beg to differ," Dr. Argent said. "Much as I am loath to say it, Your Ladyship, but I believe the girl was instrumental in the death of Lord Camden—perhaps for some real or imagined insult. Being Corsican, she would follow the rule of vendetta if she felt slighted. I conjecture that, finding him engrossed in his work as he descended the steps to find himself a midnight meal, she took the opportunity to push him."

Her Ladyship sobbed at the revelation, but Dr. Argent pressed on. "She felt the guilt of it, but also, I suspect, delighted in her power over Your Ladyship and decided to torment you with this apparition. It is even possible that we will find she has secreted objects of value in her room, which she hoped to profit from by forcing you to leave and giving her the run of the house."

"So— So then there is no ghost of my Jason in this home?" Her Ladyship asked.

"No, dear lady,' Dr. Argent said, his eyes focusing on something none of us could see. "Not of your husband, but now there *is* a presence. A hostile one. I think it is time you did leave for a while so that I may exorcise this vixen and once more bring peace to Camden House."

Teel James Glenn's stories have been printed in magazines from *Weird Tales*, *Spinetingler*, *SciFan*, *Mad*, *Black Belt*, *Fantasy Tales*, *Crimson Streets*, *Silver Blade Quarterly*, *Blazing Adventures*, and scores of other publications. He is also the winner of the 2012 Pulp Ark Award for Best Author. His website is: theurbanswashbuckler.com

THE MAN BENEATH THE STREET

by Dana Martin Batory

I'm not a detective. Or at least, not a criminal or private detective. I'm just an amateur local historian living and working in Ridgeline, Ohio. However, I must admit that my name, Valentine Snow, is not unknown to the staff at the State Historical Society in Columbus. I've cleared up more than one or two historical mysteries. So I suppose I'm sort of a detective.

Now that that is settled, my first brush with a crime took place a few years ago when Ridgeline was undergoing what was popularly termed "urban renewal."

At the time I was still living just outside town in a shabby but comfortable house dating back to the 1860s. It used to be part of a large farm that occupied two or three hundred acres on the east side. It was long ago broken up into building lots by the money-hungry heirs. The small place met most of my needs, but my reference library not only filled my place, it also spilled over into my Mom and Dad's and a brother's.

I and a few others like me called the urban renewal what it was, state sanctioned, wholesale vandalism. What little character the tiny village ever possessed was rapidly disappearing under the treads of bulldozers or the crashes of wrecking balls. Our heritage, as pitiful as it may have been, was being destroyed and the blind city officials were cheering it on. Only the pompoms, short skirts and an occasional flash of panties were missing. Hell, the founder's once magnificent home was now stacked full of used tires and the grounds were covered in acres of junk cars.

Ridgeline? It lies roughly halfway between Cleveland and Columbus. The village had been a Ohio rail center since 1851, purely due to the fact that two major lines accidentally crossed in the village, one going roughly north-south, the other roughly east-west. In its heyday hundreds of trains passed through daily. It was a busy town filled with shops, twenty-three bars, and two whorehouses.

That also explained Ridgeline's extensive rail yards and the massive brick roundhouse.

The first is a shadow of its former self and the latter was destroyed before the preservation society could purchase it. Its brick and steel were sold as scrap by its half-wit owner. For all that, the village was and still is a hick town. As a lifelong resident, I've earned the right to call it that. But don't you try it!

I stood in the front yard of old man Jackson Blean at the corner of Bucyrus Avenue and East Washington Street, just at the bottom of the big hill. A group of us gathered that hot July morning to do some sidewalk supervising and watch the old street being peeled back. In case you don't know it, it doesn't take much to amuse people in a small town.

A bright yellow front loader was busy ripping up the carefully-laid heavy Wooster paving bricks from their bed of concrete and tar, dumping them into a rumbling truck. Some of us had already managed to salvage a few as souvenirs and they stood about here and there, like small russet-red Egyptian pyramids on peoples's lawns, their glaze making them shine brightly. One ambitious guy had a couple hundred in a neat stack. A larger machine was busy digging a deep trench to install the new storm sewers.

Suddenly the front loader came to a dead stop and the clouds of fine dust began to settle. A large, still-intact "slab" of bricks and soil leaned back precariously. Duloe, the operator, stood up in his cab, yelled something to the other workers and excitedly pointed downward. They all came scurrying over, dropping their shovels. Two or three of us joined Duloe and the men at the front of the bucket to stare down into the shallow pit.

All but myself were a bit rattled at what lay stretched out in the depression. Not only had I studied physical anthropology, but in my time I've been to a few exhumations at ancient cemeteries. I've seen the rotted bottoms of coffins give way, spilling their contents. The sight of a human skeleton was nothing new to me. My only real surprise was seeing one there.

It lay on its back, its arms and legs close against the sides. The skull was tilted. A few shreds of bluish cloth covered the bones. I immediately noticed the badly rusted Smith & Wesson Model One .38 revolver and the cartridge belt and buckle sagging at its waist. My cousin and the foreman waved me forward.

I knelt between the men for a closer inspection, poking among the rib remains with an index finger and picked up a small button from among the ribs. Brushing away the corrosion on my blue jeans, I could barely made out the letters "RPD."

Silently urged on by the rest, I gently eased the skull away from the spinal column and slowly rotated it in my hands. In the center of its forehead was a neat round hole. Dirt and sand gushed from the brain case and one of the workers looked sick. The entire back of the skull had been blown away.

I carefully replaced the skull and passed a quick semi-professional eye over the remains. Suddenly someone was rudely pushing through the on-lookers, grunting "Out of the way. Out of the way." One man was nearly shoved backwards into the bucket. Naturally, some busybody had seen fit to call the police. Why can't people mind their own damn business?

Overweight with both flesh and equipment, Police Chief "Pukey" Pewsey stood barely balanced at the grave's rim. The skeleton dumbfounded him for a moment, but he quickly sized up the situation, being the professional he was, and decided it was a perfect opportunity to show his authority.

"Get out of there, you." He must have meant me. A fat hand grabbed the back of my shirt and I was pushed, stumbling, to the sandstone curb.

"No need to get rough," I observed, rubbing my arm.

"Shut up, Snow, or I'll run you in for interfering with a police investigation and causing a disturbance at an emergency. Maybe even resisting arrest. We've had trouble with you before. In fact, I want all of you people out of here. Now! You construction workers can stay. We'll want to talk to you."

We silently retreated about twenty feet away, to the shaded comfort and safety of Mr. Blean's front porch, to watch the proceedings. Someone had a digital camera out.

Pewsey was deliberating trying to escalate a minor situation into something serious. He stormed towards the wooden steps. "I said get out of here. That means go home. H. O. M. E."

No one moved. Perhaps we were surprised that Pukey knew how to spell. Pewsey muttered something into his radio and began stomping up the steps.

"I said go! Or I'll run all of you in for disobeying a direct police command."

"We're not bothering you," said someone.

By that time, the furious Pewsey was on the porch and reaching for his taser. No one defied a direct order from him.

That's when Mr. Blean stepped forward. "These gentlemen are my invited guests. When you buy the place, Pukey, then you can say who stays and goes. Until then, shut your big fat mouth and get the hell off my porch or I'll take whatever steps are necessary to get you off. And then I'll contact my son's law firm in Cleveland and sue your lard ass."

We were a law-abiding bunch of young guys, but it was obvious to Pewsey that it wouldn't be smart—in more ways than one—to assault the frail eighty-five-year-old man. The taser stayed in its holster.

"I'll talk to you later," Pewsey screamed at Blean. His dramatic exit was spoiled when he slipped going down the steps and nearly fell on his face. We all sniggered.

"I look forward to it," Mr. Blean replied calmly. "I could use another good laugh and a nice settlement from the village's insurance company."

All four cruisers were now parked along the street and their occupants were stringing up yellow tape, interviewing the workers, measuring, photographing, and trying to look busy, greedily racking up the overtime. The county coroner soon rolled up, briefly disappeared behind the slab, and an olive drab tent was quickly erected over the grisly discovery. On his heels followed my friends Taggart and Higgs, a TV reporter and a cameraman from the nearby city of Ladsfield, and Sally Rees, a reporter for its newspaper.

They attempted asking a few questions and were brushed off. Higgs shot some footage of Taggart standing in front of the disorganized commotion around the site. They then headed towards us. By that time, the show was basically over and only Mr. Blean and I were left on the porch.

"Valentine, old buddy," said Taggart. "Sutton told me to talk to you. Chief Pukey said he couldn't give a statement or answer any questions until they make a thorough investigation. Maybe not for two or three days. Seeing how you got a chance to examine the remains, maybe you can make some observations."

"I only had a few minutes before I was thrown out," I said. "But I saw enough. The construction crew uncovered the skeleton while digging up the street. It was buried in a shallow grave scooped out just beneath the bricks. It belongs to a male, probably in his late twenties or thirties. The buttons and weapon indicate he was a member of the old Ridgeline Police Department. A hole in the skull indicates he was shot through the forehead by a heavy caliber bullet, probably from an Army Colt .44 revolver. Not a suicide. Not a robbery. I saw four silver dollars and a gold piece in the dirt. It was murder. And the street was put down in September 1898."

"He's been down there over a hundred years?" asked Taggart.

"Sure looks like it," I answered.

Taggart naturally asked too many questions while Higgs shot way too much footage, assuring that the studio would have plenty of raw material to edit into a three-minute time block. Then Sally asked some follow-up questions. I must admit, I do enjoy seeing myself on TV and being quoted in the newspapers.

✗   ✗   ✗   ✗

Five days later, Police Chief Pewsey held a news conference and read a brief press release. I summarize the highlights.

"After intensive investigation by the Ridgeline Police Department, assisted by the county sheriff's department and the FBI, we have established that the skeleton found beneath East Washington Street last week was that of a male adult, probably in his late twenties or thirties. The uniform buttons and the service revolver indicate he was a member of the Ridgeline Police Department. He died from a single gunshot wound, the bullet entering through the forehead and exiting at the rear. Probably of forty-four caliber. The date of death is thought to be in the early 1890s. Perhaps 1891 or 1892, but the coroner can't be more specific. Unfortunately, city records and newspaper files from that time period are incomplete.

"A thorough examination of what documents still exist did not report a missing Ridgeline police officer. The department has even sought the expertise of all *important* local historians with no results.

"As fellow police officers it truly saddens us that not only was a brother officer brutally murdered, but he then was buried like some kind of a dead animal. Though his honored name is known but to God, the city of Ridgeline will bury the fine hero with all the honors due to a law enforcement officer ruthlessly gunned down in the line of duty. Unfortunately, his cowardly murderer now remains beyond our laws, but we are certain a much higher court has pronounced sentence."

It's always nice to have oneself proved right. I ignored the petty "all the important local historians" jab, considering the jackass who mouthed the words.

✗　✗　✗　✗

The mystery skeleton was the biggest thing to hit Ridgeline since the draft riots of 1862, when Federal troops were sent in. A close second was the "Great Labor Uprising of 1877" that spread through the state. Enthusiastic Ridgeliners had joined in and blocked the railroad tracks.

I love a mystery, especially a historical mystery, and I was already busy searching for the identity of the dead man. Surrounded by stacks of newspapers, documents, diaries, and journals, I realized Pewsey was right about one thing: written documents were getting me nowhere.

Besides my own extensive files on local history, which vastly exceeded those of any other individual or institution, I made it a point to keep track of the older residents of the city and county.

So, like a good detective, I began following up my leads. My best source for oral history had always been Roger Powys, who was pushing ninety. He answered my questions during the TV commercials while sitting in the nursing home's common room.

"Eighteen ninety-eight? That's a bit before my time, Val. Just how old do you think I am? Wait a minute. Have you tried old man Routledge? Never heard of him before? I don't wonder. Keeps to himself. Always did. He's older than the hills. He's in the book."

I was surprised to find Bill Routledge living almost under my nose. The family operated an organic produce farm just outside town. I drove out on the chance he would know something.

When I pulled in, an old man was bent over, pulling weeds in a large, well-groomed vegetable garden. He looked up and shaded his eyes against the sun. He looked well over ninety. That had to be my man.

I introduced myself. "Mr. Routledge, I'm Valentine Snow, a local historian. I'm looking into the story behind the skeleton they found under the street: the policeman killed around 1898."

"I'm Bill Routledge, Junior," the old man laughed. "You want my dad. He's on the back porch snapping green beans."

I followed his finger. Bill Senior sat hunched over in a ladder-back chair. He looked like a wet washcloth that had been wrung out and left to dry in the sun. I never saw a man so wrinkled before or since. He was a living raisin. His eyes, however, were sharp and clear and so was his mind, I soon discovered.

Once again, I introduced myself and explained my mission.

Routledge never paused in snapping his green beans. His nimble fingers fed them like a machine-gun into the large galvanized bucket at his feet and dropped the nubs into a cardboard box.

"I'll be 114 next year," he said right off. "My paw lived to 115. I'm hoping to break his record. So, they finally found the damn mick, did they? Sure as Hell took 'em long enough. Everybody thought he'd skipped town on a boxcar."

"You know who it is?" I asked.

"Yep. Joe O'Malley. Knew him well. Redheaded Irishman. Good Catholic." He snickered at the word "good" and went on. "Twelve brats and a wife nearly as dumb as he was. She had a tongue that could strip paint off a wall.

"O'Malley was the meanest, dirtiest cop that ever walked a beat. Yellow-bellied loud-mouthed coward and bully. Big as an ox and just a tad smarter. His only qualification was wanting the job. Loved it. Was always knocking smaller folks and kids around. Real tough."

I knew we were off to a good start. "Do you know what actually happened?" I asked. I pulled up another chair and began snapping beans alongside him. I hoped Routledge would remain talkative.

"Well, I knows of one story."

"I'd love to hear it," I urged.

"It's a long un," he warned.

"No problem, Mr. Routledge," I answered. "My time is my own."

"Okay. It all started one day in the rail yards. I was about fourteen years old at the time. Tom Tiverton was head of a section gang working on a new spur to the Evans Feed Mill. He was a big,

big man. Tough as nails but easy-going. Good-natured. Too good-natured. I was sitting on a pile of cross ties watching 'em drive spikes. Never could understand how they kept from getting their mauls all tangled up.

"O'Malley strutted by in his clean uniform and shiny buttons. He loved that costume. He was pushing along some kid hobo he just rousted from an empty freight car. He couldn't have been much older than me. From the bruises, swollen eyes, and blood, we knew O'Malley had been amusing himself with his fists and his billy club. The poor kid almost fell to the ground and O'Malley gave him a smack up aside the head with his fist. I remember the kid cried like a little baby.

"'That'll be enough of that,' said Tom in an ice-cold voice. 'Hit him again, O'Malley, and you'll deal with me.'

"'You mind your own damn business, Tiverton,' O'Malley sneered back. 'High time this little punk was taught to respect the law. When I say "move," you move. Nine years old or ninety, nobody back-talks me. And that goes for you, too.'

"'Like I said,' warned Tiverton. 'Lay off.'

"Just to show him who was boss, O'Malley gave the kid a punch in the belly that sent him into a wet ditch. One of the gang went down to help him. The rest stood around waiting for it. It came. Tom never said a word. His ham of a fist lifted O'Malley off his feet and knocked him into the ballast. I remember O'Malley's pretty uniform was all covered in dirt and cinders.

"'You dirty son-of-a-bitch!' O'Malley hollered from the ground. And he pulled out his revolver.

"Tom brought his boot down on O'Malley's wrist and took the gun away just like a rattle from a baby. He tossed it over his shoulder to one of the gang and jerked O'Malley to feet. Then he gave him a kick in the rear that sent him six feet down the tracks.

"'Git out of here,' he ordered O'Malley. 'You can pick your gun up at the mayor's office. And I'll be sure to tell him why I took it.'

"He got, while the bunch of us gave him a good horselaugh. The gang passed the hat for the kid, gave him some food from their lunch pails, and saw him safely off in a outgoing boxcar."

"Tom thought that was the end of it, but not me. As far as he was concerned, it had been more than a fair fight. I knew trouble was a-coming. O'Malley wouldn't forget. I figured on an ambush in an alley one dark night and a first-class beating. We was all surprised when the police chief told his maw that Tom's body was down at the undertaker's."

"What happened?" I asked, my hands frozen in mid-bean.

"O'Malley and his brother-in-law Mike said they'd caught Tom stealing whiskey from a boxcar in the yards late the night before. Tom put up a struggle and come at 'em with a knife. They'd been obliged to shoot him. The undertaker told me he counted fifteen bullet holes."

"Fifteen!" I exclaimed. "Two men each with a revolver, that means …"

Routledge interrupted me. "Yeah. One of 'em must've reloaded and pumped in some more. They had an inquest. Ruled 'justified.' Someone mentioned all the wounds. O'Malley said Tilverton just kept on coming. He was just a big guy who took a lot of killing. Why it is folk always take the cops' side?"

"Stupidity, I guess," was my only answer. Who does know?

"Well, we all knows what really happened. O'Malley and Mike gunned him down in cold blood while he was alone in the yard cleaning a switch. Couldn't prove it, of course.

"A few days later Tom's section gang found what was left of young Mike lying across the tracks. Head on one side. Feet on the other. Body in between. He stunk like whiskey. Everybody figured he got fallen-down drunk for real.

"Well, O'Malley must have had other thoughts, like maybe he'd been pushed. He tried mighty hard to stick close to town at night after that. I heard tell that he was checking train schedules and closed his bank account. Like he was getting ready to do a skip.

"One day, he was just plain gone. He'd gone out on his night shift to check the yards and never come back. They did find his bowler hat in the yards. Everybody figured he'd lost it jumping a freight to get away from his wife and kids. The authorities made a big search for him. Telegraphed up and down all the lines. Finally gave up. So did his wife. Packed up all the red-headed brats and went back East."

"All very interesting, Mr. Routledge," I observed. "So how did he end up under the street?"

"I'm gitting to that. Seems O'Malley never left town at night to check the yards. Just said he did. He was too scared. He kept a-thinking about Mike.

"While he was walking past the street construction, someone stepped out and blasted him with an old .44 Army Colt. He dumped the carcass into a shallow grave dug in the roadbed, shoveled on some dirt, tamped it down good and firm, and smoothed it out real nice. He then lost the bowler at the yards."

"It does fit the facts, Mr. Routledge," I agreed. "But how do you know so much?"

"Simple, Mr. Valentine. I killed the son-of-a-bitch. Tom Tiverton was my step-brother."

✗ ✗ ✗ ✗

Routledge Senior passed away quietly in his sleep at home after beating his father's record by two years. I attended the quiet ceremony. Occasionally when I'm doing genealogical research at the cemetery, I visit his well-kept grave. But after the town's big ceremony, the twenty-one gun salute and the fine words, the grave of the unknown policeman remains unvisited and uncared for, his name still unknown, but to the Devil.

And Police Chief "Pukey" Pewsey? He disappeared one day. Rumor has it that he tried molesting the wrong underage girl and her relatives made Ridgeline too hot for him. Strange that he disappeared just before they finished repaving East Washington Street.

✗

Dana Martin Batory is a freelance writer and cabinetmaker who also restores vintage machinery. His essays have been published in *The Armchair Detective*, *The Baker Street Journal*, and *The Sherlock Holmes Journal*, and he is the author of *The Federation Holmes*, *A Baker Street Dozen+*, and *Dreams of Future Past*.

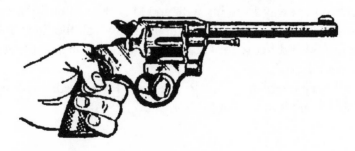

THE ADVENTURE OF THE CROOKED MAN

by Sir Arthur Conan Doyle

One summer night, a few months after my marriage, I was seated by my own hearth smoking a last pipe and nodding over a novel, for my day's work had been an exhausting one. My wife had already gone upstairs, and the sound of the locking of the hall door some time before told me that the servants had also retired. I had risen from my seat and was knocking out the ashes of my pipe when I suddenly heard the clang of the bell.

I looked at the clock. It was a quarter to twelve. This could not be a visitor at so late an hour. A patient evidently, and possibly an all-night sitting. With a wry face I went out into the hall and opened the door. To my astonishment it was Sherlock Holmes who stood upon my step.

"Ah, Watson," said he, "I hoped that I might not be too late to catch you."

"My dear fellow, pray come in."

"You look surprised, and no wonder! Relieved, too, I fancy! Hum! You still smoke the Arcadia mixture of your bachelor days, then! There's no mistaking that fluffy ash upon your coat. It's easy to tell that you have been accustomed to wear a uniform, Watson. You'll never pass as a pure-bred civilian as long as you keep that habit of carrying your handkerchief in your sleeve. Could you put me up to-night?"

"With pleasure."

"You told me that you had bachelor quarters for one, and I see that you have no gentleman visitor at present. Your hat-stand proclaims as much."

"I shall be delighted if you will stay."

"Thank you. I'll fill the vacant peg then. Sorry to see that you've had the British workman in the house. He's a token of evil. Not the drains, I hope?"

"No, the gas."

"Ah! He has left two nail-marks from his boot upon your linoleum just where the light strikes it. No, thank you, I had some supper at Waterloo, but I'll smoke a pipe with you with pleasure."

I handed him my pouch, and he seated himself opposite to me and smoked for some time in silence. I was well aware that nothing but business of importance would have brought him to me at such an hour, so I waited patiently until he should come round to it.

"I see that you are professionally rather busy just now," said he, glancing very keenly across at me.

"Yes, I've had a busy day," I answered. "It may seem very foolish in your eyes," I added, "but really I don't know how you deduced it."

Holmes chuckled to himself. "I have the advantage of knowing your habits, my dear Watson," said he. "When your round is a short one you walk, and when it is a long one you use a hansom. As I perceive that your boots, although used, are by no means dirty, I cannot doubt that you are at present busy enough to justify the hansom."

"Excellent!" I cried.

"Elementary," said he. "It is one of those instances where the reasoner can produce an effect which seems remarkable to his neighbour, because the latter has missed the one little point which is the basis of the deduction. The same may be said, my dear fellow, for the effect of some of these little sketches of yours, which is entirely meretricious, depending as it does upon your retaining in your own hands some factors in the problem which are never imparted to the reader. Now, at present I am in the position of these same readers, for I hold in this hand several threads of one of the strangest cases which ever perplexed a man's brain, and yet I lack the one or two which are needful to complete my theory. But I'll have them, Watson, I'll have them!" His eyes kindled and a slight flush sprang into his thin cheeks. For an instant the veil had lifted upon his keen, intense nature, but for an instant only. When I glanced again his face had resumed that red-Indian composure which had made so many regard him as a machine rather than a man.

"The problem presents features of interest," said he. "I may even say exceptional features of interest. I have already looked into the matter, and have come, as I think, within sight of my solution. If you could accompany me in that last step you might be of considerable service to me."

"I should be delighted."

"Could you go as far as Aldershot to-morrow?"

"I have no doubt Jackson would take my practice."

"Very good. I want to start by the 11:10 from Waterloo."

"That would give me time."

"Then, if you are not too sleepy, I will give you a sketch of what has happened, and of what remains to be done."

"I was sleepy before you came. I am quite wakeful now."

"I will compress the story as far as may be done without omitting anything vital to the case. It is conceivable that you may even have read some account of the matter. It is the supposed murder of Colonel Barclay, of the Royal Munsters, at Aldershot, which I am investigating."

"I have heard nothing of it."

"It has not excited much attention yet, except locally. The facts are only two days old. Briefly they are these:

"The Royal Munsters is, as you know, one of the most famous Irish regiments in the British Army. It did wonders both in the Crimea and the Mutiny, and has since that time distinguished itself upon every possible occasion. It was commanded up to Monday night by James Barclay, a gallant veteran, who started as a full private, was raised to commissioned rank for his bravery at the time of the Mutiny, and so lived to command the regiment in which he had once carried a musket.

"Colonel Barclay had married at the time when he was a sergeant, and his wife, whose maiden name was Miss Nancy Devoy, was the daughter of a former colour-sergeant in the same corps. There was, therefore, as can be imagined, some little social friction when the young couple (for they were still young) found themselves in their new surroundings. They appear, however, to have quickly adapted themselves, and Mrs Barclay has always, I understand, been as popular with the ladies of the regiment as her husband was with his brother officers. I may add that she was a woman of great beauty, and that even now, when she has been married for upward of thirty years, she is still of a striking and queenly appearance.

"Colonel Barclay's family life appears to have been a uniformly happy one. Major Murphy, to whom I owe most of my facts, assures me that he has never heard of any misunderstanding between the pair. On the whole, he thinks that Barclay's devotion to his wife was greater than his wife's to Barclay. He was acutely uneasy if he were absent from her for a day. She, on the other hand, though devoted and faithful, was less obtrusively affectionate. But they were regarded in the regiment as the very model of a middle-aged couple. There was absolutely nothing in their mutual relations to prepare people for the tragedy which was to follow.

"Colonel Barclay himself seems to have had some singular traits in his character. He was a dashing, jovial old soldier in his usual mood, but there were occasions on which he seemed to show himself capable of considerable violence and vindictiveness. This side of his nature, however, appears never to have been turned towards his wife. Another fact which had struck Major Murphy and three out of five of the other officers with whom I conversed was the singular sort of depression which came upon him at times. As the major expressed it, the smile has often been struck from his mouth, as if by some invisible hand, when he has been joining in the gaieties and chaff of the mess-table. For days on end, when the mood was on him, he has been sunk in the deepest gloom. This and a certain tinge of superstition were the only unusual traits in his character which his brother officers had observed. The latter peculiarity took the form of a dislike to being left alone, especially after dark. This puerile feature in a nature which was conspicuously manly had often given rise to comment and conjecture.

"The first battalion of the Royal Munsters (which is the old One Hundred and Seventeenth) has been stationed at Aldershot for some years. The married officers live out of barracks, and the colonel has during all this time occupied a villa called 'Lachine,' about half a mile from the north camp. The house stands in its own grounds, but the west side of it is not more than thirty yards from the highroad. A coachman and two maids form the staff of servants. These with their master and mistress were the sole occupants of Lachine, for the Barclays had no children, nor was it usual for them to have resident visitors.

"Now for the events at Lachine between nine and ten on the evening of last Monday.

"Mrs Barclay was, it appears, a member of the Roman Catholic Church and had interested herself very much in the establishment of the Guild of St George, which was formed in connection with the Watt Street Chapel for the purpose of supplying the poor with cast-off clothing. A meeting of the Guild had been held that evening at eight, and Mrs Barclay had hurried over her dinner in order to be present at it. When leaving the house she was heard by the coachman to make some commonplace remark to her husband, and to assure him that she would be back before very long. She then called for Miss Morrison, a young lady who lives in the next villa and the two went off together to their meeting. It lasted forty minutes, and at a quarter-past nine Mrs Barclay returned home, having left Miss Morrison at her door as she passed.

"There is a room which is used as a morning-room at Lachine. This faces the road and opens by a large glass folding-door on to the lawn. The lawn is thirty yards across and is only divided from the highway by a low wall with an iron rail above it. It was into this room that Mrs Barclay went upon her return. The blinds were not down, for the room was seldom used in the evening, but Mrs Barclay herself lit the lamp and then rang the bell, asking Jane Stewart, the housemaid, to bring her a cup of tea, which was quite contrary to her usual habits. The colonel had been sitting in the dining-room, but, hearing that his wife had returned, he joined her in the morning-room. The coachman saw him cross the hall and enter it. He was never seen again alive.

"The tea which had been ordered was brought up at the end of ten minutes; but the maid, as she approached the door, was surprised to hear the voices of her master and mistress in furious altercation. She knocked without receiving any answer, and even turned the handle, but only to find that the door was locked upon the inside. Naturally enough she ran down to tell the cook, and the two women with the coachman came up into the hall and listened to the dispute which was still raging. They all agreed that only two voices were to be heard, those of Barclay and of his wife. Barclay's remarks were subdued and abrupt so that none of them were audible to the listeners. The lady's, on the other hand, were most bitter, and when she raised her voice could be plainly heard. 'You coward!' she repeated over and over again. 'What can be done now? What can be done now? Give me back my life. I will never so much as breathe the same air with you again! You coward! You coward!' Those were scraps of her conversation, ending in a sudden dreadful cry in the man's voice, with a crash, and a piercing scream from the woman. Convinced that some tragedy had occurred, the coachman rushed to the door and strove to force it, while scream after scream issued from within. He was unable, however, to make his way in, and the maids were too distracted with fear to be of any assistance to him. A sudden thought struck him, however, and he ran through the hall door and round to the lawn upon which the long French windows open. One side of the window was open, which I understand was quite usual in the summertime, and he passed without difficulty into the room. His mistress had ceased to scream and was stretched insensible upon a couch, while with his feet tilted over the side of an armchair, and his head upon the ground near the corner of the fender, was lying the unfortunate soldier stone dead in a pool of his own blood.

"Naturally, the coachman's first thought, on finding that he could do nothing for his master, was to open the door. But here an unexpected and singular difficulty presented itself. The key was not in the inner side of the door, nor could he find it anywhere in the room. He went out again, therefore, through the window, and, having obtained the help of a policeman and of a medical man, he returned. The lady, against whom naturally the strongest suspicion rested, was removed to her room, still in a state of insensibility. The colonel's body was then placed upon the sofa and a careful examination made of the scene of the tragedy.

"The injury from which the unfortunate veteran was suffering was found to be a jagged cut some two inches long at the back part of his head, which had evidently been caused by a violent blow from a blunt weapon. Nor was it difficult to guess what that weapon may have been. Upon the floor, close to the body, was lying a singular club of hard carved wood with a bone handle. The colonel possessed a varied collection of weapons brought from the different countries in which he had fought, and it is conjectured by the police that this club was among his trophies. The servants deny having seen it before, but among the numerous curiosities in the house it is possible that it may have been overlooked. Nothing else of importance was discovered in the room by the police, save the inexplicable fact that neither upon Mrs Barclay's person nor upon that of the victim nor in any part of the room was the missing key to be found. The door had eventually to be opened by a locksmith from Aldershot.

"That was the state of things, Watson, when upon the Tuesday morning I, at the request of Major Murphy, went down to Aldershot to supplement the efforts of the police. I think that you will acknowledge that the problem was already one of interest, but my observations soon made me realize that it was in truth much more extraordinary than would at first sight appear.

"Before examining the room I cross-questioned the servants, but only succeeded in eliciting the facts which I have already stated. One other detail of interest was remembered by Jane Stewart, the housemaid. You will remember that on hearing the sound of the quarrel she descended and returned with the other servants. On that first occasion, when she was alone, she says that the voices of her master and mistress were sunk so low that she could hardly hear anything, and judged by their tones rather than their words that they had fallen out. On my pressing her, however, she remembered that she heard the word David uttered twice by the lady. The point is of the utmost importance as guiding us towards the reason of the sudden quarrel. The colonel's name, you remember, was James.

"There was one thing in the case which had made the deepest impression both upon the servants and the police. This was the contortion of the colonel's face. It had set, according to their account, into the most dreadful expression of fear and horror which a human countenance is capable of assuming. More than one person fainted at the mere sight of him, so terrible was the effect. It was quite certain that he had foreseen his fate, and that it had caused him the utmost horror. This, of course, fitted in well enough with the police theory, if the colonel could have seen his wife making a murderous attack upon him. Nor was the fact of the wound being on the back of his head a fatal objection to this, as he might have turned to avoid the blow. No information could be got from the lady herself, who was temporarily insane from an acute attack of brain-fever.

"From the police I learned that Miss Morrison, who you remember went out that evening with Mrs Barclay, denied having any knowledge of what it was which had caused the ill-humour in which her companion had returned.

"Having gathered these facts, Watson, I smoked several pipes over them, trying to separate those which were crucial from others which were merely incidental. There could be no question that the most distinctive and suggestive point in the case was the singular disappearance of the door-key. A most careful search had failed to discover it in the room. Therefore it must have been taken from it. But neither the colonel nor the colonel's wife could have taken it. That was perfectly clear. Therefore a third person must have entered the room. And that third person could only have come in through the window. It seemed to me that a careful examination of the room and the lawn might possibly reveal some traces of this mysterious individual. You know my methods, Watson. There was not one of them which I did not apply to the inquiry. And it ended by my discovering traces, but very different ones from those which I had expected. There had been a man in the room, and he had crossed the lawn coming from the road. I was able to obtain five very clear impressions of his footmarks: one in the roadway itself, at the point where he had climbed the low wall, two on the lawn, and two very faint ones upon the stained boards near the window where he had entered. He had apparently rushed across the lawn, for his toe-marks were much deeper than his heels. But it was not the man who surprised me. It was his companion."

"His companion!"

Holmes pulled a large sheet of tissue-paper out of his pocket and carefully unfolded it upon his knee.

"What do you make of that?" he asked.

The paper was covered with the tracings of the footmarks of some small animal. It had five well-marked footpads, an indication of long nails, and the whole print might be nearly as large as a dessert-spoon.

"It's a dog," said I.

"Did you ever hear of a dog running up a curtain? I found distinct traces that this creature had done so."

"A monkey, then?"

"But it is not the print of a monkey."

"What can it be, then?"

"Neither dog nor cat nor monkey nor any creature that we are familiar with. I have tried to reconstruct it from the measurements. Here are four prints where the beast has been standing motionless.

You see that it is no less than fifteen inches from fore-foot to hind. Add to that the length of neck and head, and you get a creature not much less than two feet long—probably more if there is any tail. But now observe this other measurement. The animal has been moving, and we have the length of its stride. In each case it is only about three inches. You have an indication, you see, of a long body with very short legs attached to it. It has not been considerate enough to leave any of its hair behind it. But its general shape must be what I have indicated, and it can run up a curtain. and it is carnivorous."

"How do you deduce that?"

"Because it ran up the curtain. A canary's cage was hanging in the window, and its aim seems to have been to get at the bird."

"Then what was the beast?"

"Ah, if I could give it a name it might go a long way towards solving the case. On the whole, it was probably some creature of the weasel and stoat tribe—and yet it is larger than any of these that I have seen."

"But what had it to do with the crime?"

"That, also, is still obscure. But we have learned a good deal, you perceive. We know that a man stood in the road looking at the quarrel between the Barclays—the blinds were up and the room lighted. We know, also, that he ran across the lawn, entered the room, accompanied by a strange animal, and that he either struck the colonel or, as is equally possible, that the colonel fell down from sheer fright at the sight of him, and cut his head on the corner of the fender. Finally we have the curious fact that the intruder carried away the key with him when he left."

"Your discoveries seem to have left the business more obscure than it was before," said I.

"Quite so. They undoubtedly showed that the affair was much deeper than was at first conjectured. I thought the matter over, and I came to the conclusion that I must approach the case from another aspect. But really, Watson, I am keeping you up, and I might just as well tell you all this on our way to Aldershot to-morrow."

"Thank you, you have gone rather too far to stop."

"It is quite certain that when Mrs Barclay left the house at half-past seven she was on good terms with her husband. She was never, as I think I have said, ostentatiously affectionate, but she was heard by the coachman chatting with the colonel in a friendly fashion. Now, it was equally certain that, immediately on her return, she had gone to the room in which she was least likely to see her husband, had flown to tea as an agitated woman will, and finally, on his coming in to her, had broken into violent recriminations. Therefore something had occurred between seven-thirty and nine o'clock which had completely altered her feelings towards him. But Miss Morrison had been with her during the whole of that hour and a half. It was absolutely certain, therefore, in spite of her denial, that she must know something of the matter.

"My first conjecture was that possibly there had been some passages between this young lady and the old soldier, which the former had now confessed to the wife. That would account for the angry return, and also for the girl's denial that anything had occurred. Nor would it be entirely incompatible with most of the words overheard. But there was the reference to David, and there was the known affection of the colonel for his wife to weigh against it, to say nothing of the tragic intrusion of this other man, which might, of course, be entirely disconnected with what had gone before. It was not easy to pick one's steps, but, on the whole, I was inclined to dismiss the idea that there had been anything between the colonel and Miss Morrison, but more than ever convinced that the young lady held the clue as to what it was which had turned Mrs Barclay to hatred of her husband. I took the obvious course, therefore, of calling upon Miss M, of explaining to her that I was perfectly certain that she held the facts in her possession, and of assuring her that her friend, Mrs Barclay, might find herself in the dock upon a capital charge unless the matter were cleared up.

"Miss Morrison is a little ethereal slip of a girl, with timid eyes and blond hair, but I found her by no means wanting in shrewdness and common sense. She sat thinking for some time after I had spoken, and then, turning to me with a brisk air of resolution, she broke into a remarkable statement which I will condense for your benefit.

"'I promised my friend that I would say nothing of the matter, and a promise is a promise,' said she; 'but if I can really help her when so serious a charge is laid against her, and when her own mouth, poor darling, is closed by illness, then I think I am absolved from my promise. I will tell you exactly what happened upon Monday evening.

"'We were returning from the Watt Street Mission about a quarter to nine o'clock. On our way we had to pass through Hudson Street, which is a very quiet thoroughfare. There is only one lamp in it, upon the left-hand side, and as we approached this lamp I saw a man coming towards us with his back very bent, and something like a box slung over one of his shoulders. He appeared to be deformed, for he carried his head low and walked with his knees bent. We were passing him when he raised his face to look at us in the circle of light thrown by the lamp, and as he did so he stopped and screamed out in a dreadful voice, "My God, it's Nancy!" Mrs Barclay turned as white as death and would have fallen down had the dreadful-looking creature not caught hold of her. I was going to call for the police, but she, to my surprise, spoke quite civilly to the fellow.

"''I thought you had been dead this thirty years, Henry," said she in a shaking voice.

"''So I have," said he, and it was awful to hear the tones that he said it in. He had a very dark, fearsome face, and a gleam in his eyes that comes back to me in my dreams. His hair and whiskers were shot with gray, and his face was all crinkled and puckered like a withered apple.

"''Just walk on a little way, dear," said Mrs Barclay; "I want to have a word with this man. There is nothing to be afraid of." She tried to speak boldly, but she was still deadly pale and could hardly get her words out for the trembling of her lips.

"'I did as she asked me, and they talked together for a few minutes. Then she came down the street with her eyes blazing, and I saw the crippled wretch standing by the lamp-post and shaking his clenched fists in the air as if he were mad with rage. She never said a word until we were at the door here, when she took me by the hand and begged me to tell no one what had happened.

"''It's an old acquaintance of mine who has come down in the world," said she. When I promised her I would say nothing she kissed me, and I have never seen her since. I have told you now the whole truth, and if I withheld it from the police it is because I did not realize then the danger in which my dear friend stood. I know that it can only be to her advantage that everything should be known.'

"There was her statement, Watson, and to me, as you can imagine, it was like a light on a dark night. Everything which had been disconnected before began at once to assume its true place, and I had a shadowy presentiment of the whole sequence of events. My next step obviously was to find the man who had produced such a remarkable impression upon Mrs Barclay. If he were still in Aldershot it should not be a very difficult matter. There are not such a very great number of civilians, and a deformed man was sure to have attracted attention. I spent a day in the search, and by evening—this very evening, Watson—I had run him down. The man's name is Henry Wood, and he lives in lodgings in this same street in which the ladies met him. He has only been five days in the place. In the character of a registration-agent I had a most interesting gossip with his landlady. The man is by trade a conjurer and performer, going round the canteens after nightfall, and giving a little entertainment at each. He carries some creature about with him in that box, about which the landlady seemed to be in considerable trepidation, for she had never seen an animal like it. He uses it in some of his tricks according to her account. So much the woman was able to tell me, and also that it was a wonder the man lived, seeing how twisted he was, and that he spoke in a strange tongue sometimes, and that for the last two nights she had heard him groaning and weeping in his bedroom. He was all right, as far as money went, but in his deposit he had given her what looked like a bad florin. She showed it to me, Watson, and it was an Indian rupee.

"So now, my dear fellow, you see exactly how we stand and why it is I want you. It is perfectly plain that after the ladies parted from this man he followed them at a distance, that he saw the quarrel between husband and wife through the window, that he rushed in, and that the creature which he carried in his box got loose. That is all very certain. But he is the only person in this world who can tell us exactly what happened in that room."

"And you intend to ask him?"

"Most certainly—but in the presence of a witness."

"And I am the witness?"

"If you will be so good. If he can clear the matter up, well and good. If he refuses, we have no alternative but to apply for a warrant."

"But how do you know he'll be there when we return?"

"You may be sure that I took some precautions. I have one of my Baker Street boys mounting guard over him who would stick to him like a burr, go where he might. We shall find him in Hudson Street to-morrow, Watson, and meanwhile I should be the criminal myself if I kept you out of bed any longer."

It was midday when we found ourselves at the scene of the tragedy, and, under my companion's guidance, we made our way at once to Hudson Street. In spite of his capacity for concealing his emotions, I could easily see that Holmes was in a state of suppressed excitement, while I was myself tingling with that half-sporting, half-intellectual pleasure which I invariably experienced when I associated myself with him in his investigations.

"This is the street," said he as we turned into a short thoroughfare lined with plain two-storied brick houses. "Ah, here is Simpson to report."

"He's in all right, Mr Holmes," cried a small street Arab, running up to us.

"Good, Simpson!" said Holmes, patting him on the head. "Come along, Watson. This is the house." He sent in his card with a message that he had come on important business, and a moment later we were face to face with the man whom we had come to see. In spite of the warm weather he was crouching over a fire, and the little room was like an oven. The man sat all twisted and huddled in his chair in a way which gave an indescribable impression of deformity; but the face which he turned towards us, though worn and swarthy, must at some time have been remarkable for its beauty. He looked suspiciously at us now out of yellow-shot, bilious eyes, and, without speaking or rising, he waved towards two chairs.

"Mr Henry Wood, late of India, I believe," said Holmes affably. "I've come over this little matter of Colonel Barclay's death."

"What should I know about that?"

"That's what I want to ascertain. You know, I suppose, that unless the matter is cleared up, Mrs Barclay, who is an old friend of yours, will in all probability be tried for murder."

The man gave a violent start.

"I don't know who you are," he cried, "nor how you come to know what you do know, but will you swear that this is true that you tell me?"

"Why, they are only waiting for her to come to her senses to arrest her."

"My God! Are you in the police yourself?"

"No."

"What business is it of yours, then?"

"It's every man's business to see justice done."

"You can take my word that she is innocent."

"Then you are guilty."

"No, I am not."

"Who killed Colonel James Barclay, then?"

"It was a just Providence that killed him. But, mind you this, that if I had knocked his brains out, as it was in my heart to do, he would have had no more than his due from my hands. If his own guilty conscience had not struck him down it is likely enough that I might have had his blood upon my soul. You want me to tell the story. Well, I don't know why I shouldn't, for there's no cause for me to be ashamed of it.

"It was in this way, sir. You see me now with my back like a camel and my ribs all awry, but there was a time when Corporal Henry Wood was the smartest man in the One Hundred and Seventeenth foot. We were in India, then, in cantonments, at a place we'll call Bhurtee. Barclay, who died the other day, was sergeant in the same company as myself, and the belle of the regiment, ay, and the finest girl that ever had the breath of life between her lips, was Nancy Devoy, the daughter of the colour sergeant. There were two men that loved her, and one that she loved, and you'll smile when you look at this poor thing huddled before the fire and hear me say that it was for my good looks that she loved me.

"Well, though I had her heart, her father was set upon her marrying Barclay. I was a harum-scarum, reckless lad, and he had had an education and was already marked for the sword-belt. But the girl held true to me, and it seemed that I would have had her when the Mutiny broke out, and all hell was loose in the country.

"We were shut up in Bhurtee, the regiment of us with half a battery of artillery, a company of Sikhs, and a lot of civilians and women-folk. There were ten thousand rebels round us, and they were as keen as a set of terriers round a rat-cage. About the second week of it our water gave out, and it was a question whether we could communicate with General Neill's column, which was moving up-country. It was our only chance, for we could not hope to fight our way out with all the women and children, so I volunteered to go out and to warn General Neill of our danger. My offer was accepted, and I talked it over with Sergeant Barclay, who was supposed to know the ground better than any other man, and who drew up a route by which I might get through the rebel lines. At ten o'clock the same night I started off upon my journey. There were a thousand lives to save, but it was of only one that I was thinking when I dropped over the wall that night.

"My way ran down a dried-up watercourse, which we hoped would screen me from the enemy's sentries; but as I crept round the corner of it I walked right into six of them, who were crouching down in the dark waiting for me. In an instant I was stunned with a blow and bound hand and foot. But the real blow was to my heart and not to my head, for as I came to and listened to as much as I could understand of their talk, I heard enough to tell me that my comrade, the very man who had arranged the way I was to take, had betrayed me by means of a native servant into the hands of the enemy.

"Well, there's no need for me to dwell on that part of it. You know now what James Barclay was capable of. Bhurtee was relieved by Neill next day, but the rebels took me away with them in their retreat, and it was many a long year before ever I saw a white face again. I was tortured and tried to get away, and was captured and tortured again. You can see for yourselves the state in which I was left. Some of them that fled into Nepal took me with them, and then afterwards I was up past Darjeeling. The hill-folk up there murdered the rebels who had me, and I became their slave for a time until I escaped; but instead of going south I had to go north, until I found myself among the Afghans. There I wandered about for many a year, and at last came back to the Punjab, where I lived mostly among the natives and picked up a living by the conjuring tricks that I had learned. What use was it for me, a wretched cripple, to go back to England or to make myself known to my old comrades? Even my wish for revenge would not make me do that. I had rather that Nancy and my old pals should think of Harry

Wood as having died with a straight back, than see him living and crawling with a stick like a chimpanzee. They never doubted that I was dead, and I meant that they never should. I heard that Barclay had married Nancy, and that he was rising rapidly in the regiment, but even that did not make me speak.

"But when one gets old one has a longing for home. For years I've been dreaming of the bright green fields and the hedges of England. At last I determined to see them before I died. I saved enough to bring me across, and then I came here where the soldiers are, for I know their ways and how to amuse them and so earn enough to keep me."

"Your narrative is most interesting," said Sherlock Holmes. "I have already heard of your meeting with Mrs Barclay, and your mutual recognition. You then, as I understand, followed her home and saw through the window an altercation between her husband and her, in which she doubtless cast his conduct to you in his teeth. Your own feelings overcame you, and you ran across the lawn and broke in upon them."

"I did, sir, and at the sight of me he looked as I have never seen a man look before, and over he went with his head on the fender. But he was dead before he fell. I read death on his face as plain as I can read that text over the fire. The bare sight of me was like a bullet through his guilty heart."

"And then?"

"Then Nancy fainted, and I caught up the key of the door from her hand, intending to unlock it and get help. But as I was doing it it seemed to me better to leave it alone and get away, for the thing might look black against me, and anyway my secret would be out if I were taken. In my haste I thrust the key into my pocket, and dropped my stick while I was chasing Teddy, who had run up the curtain. When I got him into his box, from which he had slipped, I was off as fast as I could run."

"Who's Teddy?" asked Holmes.

The man leaned over and pulled up the front of a kind of hutch in the corner. In an instant out there slipped a beautiful reddish-brown creature, thin and lithe, with the legs of a stoat, a long, thin nose, and a pair of the finest red eyes that ever I saw in an animal's head.

"It's a mongoose," I cried.